MW01139208

MELISSA SCHROEDER

# Tangled Passions

Melissa Schroeder

Tangled Passions

First digital publication: March 2017

This is a work of fiction. Names, characters, places and incidents
either are the product of the author's imagination or are used
factiously and any resemblance to actual persons living or dead,
business establishments, events or locales is entirely

ISBN: 154113012X

ISBN-13: 978-1541130128

*Especially for Joy Harris.*

*For over a decade we have shared our love of romance stories and Hawaii 5-0, not to mention an inappropriate sense of humor that would never play well on a reality show. Les, the girls, and I will always treasure your friendship and think of you as one of the Schroeders.*

# ACKNOWLEDGMENTS

I always say that no book is ever written by one person alone. Without the support I have in my personal and professional life, I would never finish a book.

Thanks to Noelle Varner for her hard work on the edits as always, especially when my own personal chronic pain interfered. Big thanks to Brandy Walker for stepping up and creating such a beautiful cover. Thanks to the Addicts for being around for years and always supporting my publishing efforts.

And last but not least, thanks to my family for always being there.

.

**Aloha** - Hello, goodbye, love
**Bra**-Bro
**Bruddah**- brother, term of endearment
**Haole**-Newcomer to the islands
**Howzit** - How is it going?
**Kamaʻāina**-Local to the islands
**Mahalo**-Thank you
**Malasadas**- A Portuguese donut without a hole which started out as a tradition for Shrove (Fat) Tuesday. They are deep fried, dipped in sugar or cinnamon and sugar. In other words, it is a decadent treat every person must try when they go to Hawaii. If you do not try it, you fail. Do yourself a favor. Go to Leonard's and buy one. You are welcome.
**Pupule** - crazy
**Slippahs** - slippers, AKA sandals

# TANGLED PASSIONS

# CHAPTER ONE

Bright sun seared Drew Franklin's eyes as he walked out of his apartment. Monday mornings sucked. He pulled out his sunglasses and slipped them on. It was way too damned early for this, but he had no choice. Commander Martin Delano had called him to a crime scene. He hadn't wanted to drag his ass out of bed, but when the boss called, there was no way out of it.

Drew had never been a morning person. It came from nights of gaming and always having the closing shift at one of his family's restaurants. Since his shooting a year ago, he had noticed the mornings were getting harder to deal with. Granted, he was happy he was still alive, but did it have to be so fucking bright in the mornings?

Since he'd moved into the apartment several months ago, he had started walking to work. Unless it was raining, which was almost never, he enjoyed the morning walks. Well, he wouldn't say he liked them. He would say he liked his evening walks. And it had nothing to do with work. He loved working as the assistant to Task Force Hawaii's ME, Dr. Elle Middleton-McGregor. It was that *morning* thing.

Before he made it a block down the street, he saw the Task Force Hawaii's ME van barreling down the street. Elle stopped by the curb and wound down the window.

"Hey, sailor, need a ride?" she asked with a laugh.

"Only if you promise to be gentle," he said smiling. Elle was one of the best bosses he had ever had—and that included working for various family members as he had in their restaurants. He smiled, opened the door and hopped up into the van. He had barely shut the door when she took off.

"Whoa, in a hurry?"

She slanted him a look. "I want to get this over with. I haven't had any sleep thanks to this idiot." She pointed to her very rounded belly. She was in the last trimester of her pregnancy, and he knew it hadn't been easy on her. "And I will definitely have to pee by the time we get there. When the bugger isn't jumping around in my stomach, he's sitting on my bladder."

Elle was usually in a good mood for the most part, not to mention her excellent sense of humor. Lately, though, Drew knew the pregnancy was starting to wear on her.

"I think you should take the next six weeks off."

Another slanted look. "You've been talking to Graeme."

Graeme McGregor, TFH team member and newly wed to Elle, had been trying to get her to take a leave of absence for the last two months. He knew they'd had a few arguments about it.

She stuck out her chin, which was a sure sign of a brewing argument. She was a sweetie, but Elle had a definite stubborn streak, especially when talking about her abilities.

"I am *not* fragile."

Oh, boy. Elle was sweet, unless you irritated her. "No one said you were. But, you are of…" he let his voice trail off when he realized he was about to mention her age. Dammit, he had better control than that these days. Or thought he did. The lack of caffeine didn't help.

"What were you saying?" she asked, her voice just a little too sweet.

"Nothing."

"Good, because Graeme made a comment about my age last night. Stupid goat."

"He's just worried about you."

She softened. "I know. I would divorce the wanker if I didn't believe that."

"And it's nice to have someone to worry about you."

She said nothing when she came to a stoplight. Then she glanced at him.

"Are you all right?"

He hated the pity. He'd had enough of it since the shooting. "Yeah. I haven't had any coffee."

She nodded. "I know that feeling. Right now, I would kill for a big cup."

"So, where is this case located?"

"Kailua."

"Ah. And…"

"Oh, sorry." She sighed as she hit the gas. "My head is a sieve these days. Emma keeps telling me it's pregnancy hormones, and as a doctor, I understand that. But, still. Anyway, it's that case Del had looked at a few months ago. The dating service? I think we are officially taking it over."

In the last two years, there had been three murders, now four if this was one. They were all very rich men who had been involved with the same dating service, Premiere Connections.

"And calling it a serial?"

She nodded. "At least, we have to consider it."

"What's the name?"

"Uh, Branson Anderson."

"Really?"

She glanced at him. "Did you know him?"

"You know that isn't an easy question here. I'm acquainted with most of the island." In Hawaii, everyone seemed to know everyone else, or knew someone you were related to. With his family in the restaurant business, it was impossible to remember everyone you met. "But, he was a huge high school football player. Quarterback, if I remember. Back in the early nineties. He went to UCLA, then got drafted."

"He was in the NFL?"

"Well, officially, yes. He blew his knee out in his first game and it ended his career."

"You seem to know a lot about him."

"You know how it is here. Hawaiians always support each other. Hawaiians started supporting the Steelers because so many Hawaiians have played for them."

She nodded. "His maid found him this morning. I'm not sure what else."

"Damn, this is definitely going to get some attention." A murder here and there didn't always draw that much news, but a legend like Anderson was going to attract notice from the sports networks on the mainland

"Maybe that's the point."

"Yeah, well, the others got attention too. But this one will be different. A lot of people followed his career. Add in the fact that he returned and started a local business, and the TV vultures will start to circle soon. Add in meddling from the mainland, and it could get sticky."

"Definitely," she said as she started the winding road that led to Kailua. "I have a feeling Del is going to put Cat on the case."

Cat Kalakau. The TFH team member had been Drew's crush for years, but once they had a falling out, there seemed to be no going back to their friendship. They worked together, but the camaraderie they had shared was now gone. Uncomfortable silences seemed to be their only connection now. That is why he did his best to avoid her.

He glanced at his boss. There was no doubt that Elle was fishing for his feelings on the subject. "That's cool."

"Graeme actually thinks Del might give her the case to run lead on."

For a quick second, he felt a burst of pride. It was hard to ignore that feeling. Unlike many of the others, he and Cat grew up on Oahu and had known each other for years. Knowing how far she had come and how hard she had to fight to gain recognition, made the idea that she might run an entire investigation of this size even sweeter.

"That's good. She definitely deserves it."

"Yes, she does."

Elle seemed to want to talk about his relationship with Cat. He didn't want to rehash something that had started out so promising and then had fallen apart. He just wanted to move on. So, he decided to distract her.

"We don't have time to even hit a drive thru for coffee? Remember, it is Hawaii. Even McDonald's serves Kona Coffee."

"I can't have any, you know that."

"But I need some."

She glanced at him.

"And they have food."

"None of it is good for me or the baby."

"Oh, come on, Elle. Live a little."

"If we go, I don't want you to tell Graeme."

"Why not?"

"He's worried about eating fast food while I'm pregnant."

"Promise," he said crossing his heart.

She glanced over at him and laughed. "Okay."

Cat slammed her car door and hurried passed the parked vehicles and people milling in the yard. Damn, she hated being late. She was never late. For anything. *Ever.*

There were people streaming in and out of the house, and she had seen the ME van when she'd parked. Which meant that Drew was there. Everyone had arrived before her, and now she felt as if she were ten steps behind. It wasn't a position she liked to be in. She had learned early in life that if she wanted to be taken seriously, she had to work harder than men and be better at the job. Still, before joining TFH, she had never gotten the credit. Thankfully, Del was a good boss.

She located him as he stood by the body and watched Elle and Drew do their work. She tried to ignore the little hitch in her step when she saw Drew. Months after their disastrous weekend, she still felt the rush of excitement whenever she caught a glimpse of him.

"Howzit?" Del asked as she stepped up beside him.

"The traffic was a bitch. Sorry, boss."

He shook his head. "It's only going to get worse."

"Yeah. So, what happened?"

"Anderson had a date two nights ago with someone from Premiere Connections. No one had seen him since, until his cleaning service showed up this morning. Unfortunately, they cleaned the entire first floor before finding his body."

Damn. "That's going to suck."

"Yeah, but if it's like the other murders, there will be nothing."

She glanced at him from the corner of her eye. "So, we are calling it a serial?"

He nodded. "Just not to the press yet. I want to keep a lid on this. They seemed to have missed the connection with the other three. It has given us a little time to play catch up."

"Of course," she said, waiting for him to tell her what her assignment was. She was probably going to get stuck running interviews again, which she didn't mind, but it was a thankless job. People often wanted you to comfort them and she understood that. But when you did four or five interviews a day, it got a little overwhelming.

"I want you to head this one up."

For a long moment, she said nothing because his words didn't register. When Cat realized what he had said, she turned her head to look at him. He must have noticed her attention because he glanced at her.

"What?" he asked.

"You want me to take over the case? This is a serial, boss."

"Yeah, I know. I just told you that."

"This would be my first case to head up."

He nodded. "I know that. Part of it is timing. I have Marcus on that terrorism committee; and, of course, we don't know about Graeme because we don't know when Elle is going to pop."

"What a lovely visual," Elle said. "And I am not due for another six weeks."

Del looked over at her. "As long as you try to hold off until the tenth of May."

The doctor rolled her eyes. "I take it there's a bet lined up for that?"

"There's always a bet," Drew said with a smile, then he glanced in her direction and it faded. "Hey, Cat."

She nodded in return, but didn't say anything. She turned back to Del.

"You want me to head up a serial?"

He nodded. "Yeah. Adam will be overseeing the entire investigation, acting in a supervisory role. As I said, one thing is that many of us are loaded down with work. The other is that we are going to be restructuring the team. I'll talk more about it today when we have the meeting."

That was an odd turn of phrase, but she mentally shrugged it away. "Oh. Okay."

"So, you are the one on point. Of course, all the media are going to try and talk to you, and you know what to do."

"No comment for now."

"Yes. As soon as they realize we're heading up this murder, we'll get calls. They know if we are on the case, it is bigger than just one murder."

In the past two years, the press had learned when the governor assigned TFH a case, that meant it was huge. The moment media heard TFH were working a particular crime, they would go bonkers. They understood that it was the kind of case that could make their careers, if they got the inside scoop.

"Cool."

"So, Marcus and Adam have been doing a canvas, and they'll report to you what they find. Make sure you give people tasks. Delegate, or it will become too much work and overwhelm you."

"Sure thing."

"Also, I'm sure you will probably get some questions about why you were assigned to the job. Not from the team, as both Adam and I think you can handle it, and I'm sure the rest of the team does too. But being one of our younger members and least experienced, you will get hit with that question. They will insinuate that you were picked because you were a woman and our only active investigator who is a woman."

She opened her mouth but he continued.

"And partially they would be right, but it has nothing to do with quotas, it has to do with the suspect."

"We have a suspect?"

"No. But there is a higher chance this is a woman, and we need a woman who will think like one to catch her if that is true. We can do it, but I think it would be best to have you steering this case. Your perspective might help. Plus, you are a damned fine investigator. You're ready for this, and this case is tailor-made for you, I think."

"Thanks, boss."

"I have a meeting with the mayor and the governor, so I need to go. We will do a rundown of the case at two this afternoon. Sound good?"

She nodded.

"Good. See you then. Later, Elle, Drew."

They waved him off and Elle walked over to her. "Your first case to lead up. You must be so excited."

Excited...yeah. And scared out of her mind, not to mention sick to her stomach.

"I am. I just hope I can do it."

Elle shook her head. "You will, plus this team is brilliant, so you have good support."

She nodded. "Okay, can you tell me what you found?"

"More than likely he was asphyxiated. Manually."

"Like the others."

"Yes. I'll run the normal tests and, more than likely, just like the others, he had sex not too long before he was killed."

"This is going to be all over the news with it being Anderson."

"Yeah, I told Elle that," Drew said, rising to his feet. "Anderson was local grown like the others, but more entrenched. Add in being former NFL, and that's going to get a lot of attention."

"He did a lot for the community."

Drew nodded. "So, first big case?"

"Yep. Elle, do you think a woman could do this?"

She nodded. "It was with a ligature of some sort. Looks like a rope, like the others. If it was hands, it would be a dead giveaway whether it was a woman. This way, we aren't too sure."

"Oh, hey, it could be like Sea of Love with Al Pacino," Drew said.

"That was the ex in that one, wasn't it? The man she had dated before?"

"Yeah, so it could be something like that."

"True. Okay, I'm going to go talk to the guys and see if they need me, then I'm going to head back to the office."

"Good luck," Drew said.

"Thanks. I'm definitely going to need it."

He shook his head and offered her the first smile he'd given her in months. "You got this."

Then he turned back to his work. Why that comment meant more to her than Del's vote of confidence, she didn't know. With that, she turned on her heel and went in search of Marcus and Adam. She had more than enough work cut out for her and a lot to prove.

She just hoped that she didn't let everyone down.

# CHAPTER TWO

By the time Cat got back to TFH Headquarters, she needed another cup of coffee. More like a vat, really. She was usually a morning person. In fact, she liked the idea of being the first into the office. She had even beat the boss in a couple of times. But today was different. Starting off late and trying to play catch up on a minimal amount of caffeine was not productive.

The initial excitement from getting the lead in a case had worn off. The gravity of what lay ahead of her, along with the worry that she had to make a good impression, had settled in. This was her opportunity to prove that she deserved Del's respect. She would not let anything get in her way.

She grabbed her phone and stepped out of her car. The cool, comfortable morning temps were long gone. Now, the winds had died down, and she knew it was going to be a hot and sticky day. The humidity was already off the charts and without the winds, she was staring to sweat.

She didn't make it three steps before there was a reporter running toward her. Crap. She hated reporters, and she especially hated this one, Kakona Loni. They had been in school together, from kindergarten on up, and he had been a total ass then. Still was. He had dyed his hair blond, slicked it back, and thought no one knew he wore blue contacts.

She kept her head down and strode purposefully toward the door. "Detective Kalakau—"

"Agent."

"What?"

She sighed and stopped to look over at him. It made her want to punch him even more. He had been a nasty bully in high school.

"I'm an agent, not a detective, and you aren't supposed to be in this area." Until last week, they had officially been called detectives. It had changed at the request of HPD.

Kakona didn't like that. He had been pushy all those years ago, and he was pushy now. It was his job as a reporter, but it was the way he went about it that grated on her. He accused the HPD and TFH of insane cover ups. He was a conspiracy theorist, who was convinced that every cop was dirty.

"But, I wanted a quote on the Anderson case."

"No comment."

"But you don't know what I'm going to ask."

"First, you asked for a quote. Second, it doesn't matter. No comment. It is always no comment during an active investigation."

"The public has a right to know."

"Yeah, maybe, but right now, you are on state property, and without permission, I might add."

"But—"

She keyed in her code, then pulled the door open. "No more buts, just leave."

Then she had the pleasure of watching the door shut in his face.

"That is always a nice feeling," Adam said from behind her.

She turned to face the second-in-command for TFH, and gave him a smile. Adam was an island boy like her. He was truly one of the very few bald men she knew who could pull off sexy. He was huge, muscles and tats; plus, he towered over her by more than a foot. Most people would be intimidated by him, but Cat had always thought of him as comforting. There was something about having a big, bad biker as your backup.

He was about ten years her senior, but they had attended the same high school, and were probably related in some way. Where Del was always wired and ready to pop, Adam was cool and laid back. It was one of the best things about Task Force Hawaii. The yin yang of the two men in charge always kept everything running smooth.

"Especially Loni. He's an ass. Always has been one. He was annoying even in high school."

"Ah."

"Do you need something?"

He smiled. "I'm here for you. Neither Marcus nor I could find anyone who heard anything in Anderson's neighborhood."

She snorted as she punched the button for the elevator. "With those houses out there, I can see that."

"Yeah. Lots of land around there, and a lot of the people are vacation renters. Plus, you know those rich types. They would rather not talk to other folks. So, they don't pay attention to the comings and goings."

"And, they wouldn't know if something or someone was out of place."

"Also, we don't even know when the murder occurred. It could have happened last night, or the night of his date. Strangling someone doesn't always cause a lot of noise; yet, people could have been right outside and not heard a thing."

"Yeah. If it was in my neighborhood, Auntie Koko would know who spent the night."

Older women were always aunties in Hawaii, whether they were related by blood or not. It was a sign of respect, and drove home the idea of Ohana, or family.

He laughed. "You know it. Auntie Sarah was my parent's neighborhood watch commander."

She smiled, but it faded quickly. "I need to have Charity start going through the CCTV cameras, see if she can find something."

"Yeah, that's a good idea. I also want to do another roundup about the neighborhood, as soon as we get a time of death from Elle. That might give us a little more to push with by going around again."

"Elle didn't give us a time of death at the scene?"

"She said probably more than twenty-four hours."

"Well, that narrows it down."

The doors to the elevator opened and she stepped onto the lift.

"Yeah, it is kind of crappy, but we might be able to get more info to narrow that down from Elle."

"Sounds good. I'll go talk to Elle, see what insights she can give me on time of death."

"Thanks, Adam."

He was smiling at her when the doors shut. The moment she was alone, she felt the weight of responsibility. It wasn't that she didn't want to be lead investigator. She had dreamed of it for so long, Cat couldn't remember when she didn't want to take on more responsibility. But, it also meant it was her one time to prove her worth, to assure Del that he hadn't made a mistake by putting her in that position…or even hiring her in the first place. She hadn't had much experience, and he had taken a chance on her. Now, she could make sure he knew that she would not screw up.

The doors opened to reveal Charity Edwards, TFH forensics tech. The Georgia transplant was one of a kind. Her love of superheroes and vintage clothes often had her looking like a steampunk scientist one day, and Marilyn Monroe the next. She was an expert shot with a six millimeter, and made the best sweet cornbread this side of the Pacific.

"Hey," she said, smiling at Cat.

It had been a long few months to get back on common ground with Charity. She was very friendly with Drew, and had helped him recover from his injuries last year. For a long time, Cat wasn't sure if they could ever be friendly again.

"I just got in, and I am going to run tests on some of the stuff Elle sent down."

"Great. Also, I need you to do a scan of the CCTV around that neighborhood, and the roads leading in there."

"Looking for anything in particular?" Charity asked as she stepped onto the now empty elevator.

"Just anything out of the normal. We think it could be his date from this week, but it could also be someone else. An ex-lover of one of these women. So, anyone heading out of there driving erratically, anything like that."

"You got it."

The doors closed and Cat was off and running again. The need to get ahead of this pushed her on. They were already playing catch up. With three murders before this one spanning over the last eighteen months. She needed to make sure that they got up and going fast, so that they could make headway before someone else got hurt.

Adam found Elle sitting at her desk, already looking exhausted. He watched her, noting the dark circles beneath her eyes and she looked, well, uncomfortable. She took one look at his expression and scowled.

"Don't say it."

He chuckled. "I didn't say anything."

"If one more male tells me I need to rest, I might just start punching people in the throat."

"She's out for blood," Drew said. "I'm gonna grab a bite to eat now that we're done. Do you need anything?" he asked Elle.

She shook her head. "I've got a snack here."

"Be right back," he said as he hurried out the door.

"I worry about that boy," Elle said.

"Maybe all of you women here need to stop calling him a boy. He's not. He's a man."

She glanced at him, understanding lighting her eyes. "Yeah, you're right. He's changed so much in the last year since the shooting."

"Damned right he has. I know the whole lot of you like to coddle him, but he needs you to see him as a man, not a boy who needs help."

She blinked and he realized that he'd raged on about it for a while. "So, I guess you're here for the report?"

He nodded. "I take it nothing has changed?"

"No. Asphyxiation brought on by strangulation. Looks like it was another red scarf. Charity will confirm it though."

"Good. And time of death? Still no less than twenty-four hours?"

"Yeah. I'm leaning toward last night due to the lividity and body temp. Charity also has some stomach contents to study. They might help narrow down where he was and what he was doing."

"And if we can do that, who he might have been with."

"Yes," she said shifting a little.

"Are you okay?"

"Yeah," she said, resting her hand on her stomach. "This one is just sitting on my sciatic nerve, and it isn't at all comfortable."

"You should…" he trailed off at her dirty look. "What? I was going to suggest finding a massage therapist who knows how to handle prenatal massage. My cousin used one during her last pregnancy when she had the same issue."

"That is a good idea. I'll consider looking in to that."

"Cool. I can get a name for you if you want."

"I would like that. Thank you."

Then, he said nothing as he tried to come up with a way to broach the other reason he had come down.

"Was there something else?"

He sighed. "Yeah. Have you spoken to Jin?"

Jin Phillips had been through hell and back, and almost didn't make it. Now she was on the road to recovery, he just wanted to make sure she was okay.

"Haven't you talked to her?"

"We text every now and then. She...right now she says she has things to do. Mainly...herself. She said she needed to work on herself."

"Yes, but she also needs her friends."

"I take it you've talked to her?"

Elle nodded. "I'm still considered her counselor."

A year earlier, a serial killer had abducted Jin. While he had kept her hidden, the sadistic bastard had raped and tortured her. Elle had been through something similar years ago, and now counseled women.

"I just wanted to know that she's doing all right. That's all."

"She's actually getting stronger. Clean and sober now. She's talking about writing again, but I don't think she wants to do current news. You should call her."

He shook his head. "I want her to have her space. It isn't like we have a relationship anymore, but I just wanted to be sure she was still recovering."

Elle grabbed his hand and gave it a light squeeze. "She's doing well. You should ask her if she wants to get together. She's even put on weight, which is a good thing."

"Good. Thanks." He pushed those worries aside and got his mind back on the case at hand. "So, TOD within twenty-four hours, and red scarf."

His phone buzzed.

*Got the reports. Ready to get to work?* -Marcus

"Well, that's my cue. Marcus was picking up the info from HPD, talked to a few of the detectives about the other cases too. We're going to start reading over the

21

reports."

"I thought we had the reports already?"

He shook his head. "We had some, but Marcus wanted to get the detectives' input. Their observances might help, and calling makes it too easy for them to brush us off. We might be able to hunt up some of their witnesses to see if we can find a common thread."

"HPD hadn't found one yet?"

"I know, it's odd. Three different detectives apparently handled the cases. The first few were so far apart time wise, so they weren't linked. Forensics will probably connect them, but there is always a chance that friends and family members might have information that links them too. Something outside of being a client of Premiere Connections."

She nodded. "Cool. I'm waiting on the other autopsy reports. I had a copy, but I have requested the entire files."

"See ya," he said, as he turned away.

"Oh, and Adam?"

"Yeah?"

"Make sure you call Jin. I know she would like to hear from you."

He nodded and started on his way again. He knew Elle was right, but needed to make sure that he did it the right way this time. Jin had already been through too much.

Drew had waited until the last moment to make his way up to the conference room. He knew that it was a bit on the cowardly side, but it would be best if he had as little contact with Cat during this as possible.

The truth was, he knew this day was coming. Cat was beyond capable to handle the job. And he knew Del believed in helping the folks who worked for him.

Now he would be taking orders from Cat. The woman he had been in love with for years.

*Was* in love with. He had to keep remembering that. He had loved her for so long, that every now and then, he forgot about falling out of love with her. That had ended the day he had been shot.

"Hey, Drew," Charity said as she met him in the hall that lead to the conference room. "How are you doing today?"

"Doing well, and yourself?"

She smiled. "Very well, now that TJ is back on the island."

Charity's boyfriend was an FBI agent from the mainland. He'd been back visiting family for the last week.

"I'm sure Jess and Luke are happy."

She crossed her arms beneath her breasts and scowled. "Those damned traitor cats. First you, then him. They always go for the males."

He smiled, but said nothing else as he looked down the hall. He didn't want to run into Cat. It was silly. All right, she would be handling the case. He would have to have a little face-to-face time, but not much else. That way, he could keep avoiding her.

"Come on. You can sit by me."

He glanced at Charity, who offered him an understanding smile. "Stop."

"What?"

"Stop pitying me."

"Please. Pity you?" She snorted. "Darlin', you come from a family who has more restaurants on the island than there are days of the week, and even though you don't act like it, you are loaded. You should pity me."

He just shook his head and said nothing else.

"Let's go or I'll be late again." She slipped her arm through his. "I'll lose a bet if I'm the last one in there."

"Don't let Del hear you."

Their boss hated the idea that they all bet on so many things—even if he did bet on the day Elle's baby was to be born.

"Okay."

They made their way down the hall, and found the conference room half filled. Emma was sitting at the table eating. Emma was always eating. Graeme walked in through the outside door. The man was a giant, and more than once he heard Charity call him a Scottish god. He was definitely tall, but he was just big all over. The long blond hair and icy blue eyes didn't hurt the image.

"Good afternoon, everyone. Where is my bride?"

"She's on her way up. She had a phone call she had to take," Drew said.

"The woman works too hard."

"No, the woman does not," said Elle from behind him.

He turned to face her and his expression softened. "Love, you know I'm only looking out for you."

"I know and it's the only thing that's kept me from smacking you on the head, love." She gave Graeme a kiss on the cheek, then looked around. "We're waiting on Adam, Del, and Cat then?"

"They're in his office," Emma said.

Drew looked over his shoulder and saw that, indeed, Cat was with Del and the second-in-command of TFH.

"I heard they are reorganizing," Charity said. "Does anyone know what that means?"

Everyone turned to look at Emma. "What?"

"Did the boss say anything to you?"

"He was going on and on about something concerning work last night, but I was working on code."

Emma was Del's wife, who had a knack with computer programs. When she started to work on a code, she often lost track of time and tended to ignore everyone.

"And just what are you all talking about?" Del asked.

Drew turned around and found all three of them staring at them. "We wanted to know about the restructuring of our team but, apparently, Emma wasn't listening to you at all last night."

"That's nothing new. I'll go over that first and then Cat

will go over our new case. Have a seat," Del said.

It took a few moments for everyone to get seated.

"Okay, I have been talking to the governor and the mayor. Task Force Hawaii has done a lot of good in the last two years we've been operational, but they want to expand our unit. The islands are gaining more attention from many in the drug industry. You add in the issue of terrorism threats and a high priority former president who is from the islands, and the HPD are being taxed beyond what they can handle. And, truth is, they don't want to expand right now. They just hired a ton of men and women from the mainland, but what they need are a few specialized folks. That's where we come in."

"I don't like it," Emma said.

"First, I didn't ask permission, since you are working for us on contract. Secondly, you just don't like change. You'll get used to it."

Del's wife had issues with people, and she worked better in small groups.

"Still."

"Still. I'm looking more for people who will help us with certain issues, and some of them may work like you…as a contractor. I've talked with Marcus, who had to attend a meeting at Joint Base Pearl Harbor/Hickam. He's going to head up the terrorism aspect. But from that point on, I'm not sure. I just want people who know the islands and understand the issues we face. Therefore, we will be adding more people to the team."

Emma sighed and the boss ignored her.

"I'll be conducting interviews. We will continue to work the same way as we always have. We will take turns leading an investigation, but this way, we will have more people alongside us from specialized fields. The woman I'm interviewing this afternoon worked for the DEA, and grew up on the islands. She understands that side of law enforcement. Allowing us to keep most of our work in house without having to bother our liaison at HPD all the time."

"Thank God, because they are always stealing our food," Emma said.

"Emma."

She smiled.

"Okay. Now, onto the investigation. Cat. Have at it."

Cat seemed to hesitate and then she walked up to the front of the room. Drew felt his heart start to race, as it always did when he concentrated on her. It had been a year since his injuries, but he hadn't been able to get over this woman. And now he had to spend the next thirty minutes watching her give them her briefing.

Damn, he was doomed.

# CHAPTER THREE

Cat tried to swallow and found her mouth dry. It took every bit of her self control to resist the urge to dry her hands on the front of her cargo pants. She hadn't been this nervous when she made the finals of the island-wide spelling bee, or when she had gone up for her qualification as a sharp shooter. These people mattered to her more than even her own family.

"I guess we all know that we have four murders now that are probably linked. Each killed by asphyxiation, and all of them were male. They had recent dates with women from Premiere Connections."

"That's one of those dating services?" Emma asked.

"Yes. But only for rich folks. It actually showed up on the radar when they first opened, because HPD wondered if it was an escort service."

She brought it up on the big screen. "They put in a full year working on it, but they found that the business was legit. In fact, there was more than one prominent one percenter involved. Some from the mainland, some from the islands. Charity, you said you were going to look into them?"

"Yes." Charity clicked on the touch screen and brought up the website, along with a picture of the owner. "Started just under two years ago, this is one of the fastest growing businesses on the islands. According to their books, they've been running in the black since they opened, which is very odd. We would probably need a forensics accountant to make sure those reports are not fraudulent, but I'd lean on the side that they aren't. One owner, so there are no shareholders to impress with earnings."

"Why did HPD think it was an escort service?" Emma asked.

"The male members seemed to have a lot of money, while the female members were either middle class or working class. There were some rich women in there too though. At that point, HPD started watching them. It was odd that they had such a discrepancy, but apparently, it's legal. There have been a few marriages out of the entire thing," Charity said. "And then there was the fact that the Attorney General's son was a member there as well. Met his current wife."

"Current?" Cat asked. "David got married again?"

"You know the state's attorney general's son?" Del asked.

She shrugged. "School, plus, we all know each other, right Drew?"

Drew shook himself and then finally focused on her. It was that look, the one he had given her the night of Emma and Del's wedding, and she felt herself falling again. People always mistook him for a goofball, until he focused on something.

It was one of the sexiest things she had ever seen.

"Yeah. I know David, and I think that's wife number three." He looked at Del. "He can't keep it in his pants."

"Ah," he said. "Sorry, go on."

"Charity?"

"Yes. As I said, they're already operating in the black.

That is almost unheard of, even for a site that does everything over the Internet."

"They have no offices?"

"Yes, they do." Charity brought up a pic. "But, as you can tell, it's not big. They do onsite interviews, but that's all. Everything else is done over the Internet. The client makes a video and uploads it. They only go live once the client pays the...get this...five-thousand-dollar fee. That's for the guys. The ladies have a smaller fee, but I can't seem to find the amount."

"Who is the owner?" Del asked.

"Glad you asked," Charity said. She punched a few more buttons and a picture popped up. "That's her in the picture. Alice Collins is only thirty, and now has over two million dollars in net worth.

Dark blonde hair, blue eyes, and a smile that produced a set of dimples, Cat thought Collins looked like a cheerleader.

"Damn," Adam said. "Net worth?"

Charity nodded. "She has more money, and she is actually thinking of expanding to the mainland and Japan. She's careful with her money. A nice condo, a decent car, but she doesn't spend a lot of that money. She happens to be very good with investments from the looks of things."

"You got all of that already?" Cat asked.

"The HPD had a good deal of info on her already, since they thought she was running an escort business."

"Are they sure it isn't one?" Adam asked. "Sounds like one."

"Yeah, well, PC seems to be on the up and up. Actually, one of the detectives said it was run more like a matchmaking service than a dating service," Charity said.

"That would make sense that the men would pay more then," Adam said. "Reminds me of some of the matchmaking services you hear about. Is she from here?"

"Nope. She's a Cali girl, born and raised in Southern California. Both parents are now deceased, and she has no siblings. Unmarried too."

"Do you have anything else?" Cat asked.

Charity shook her head. "Elle found a few fibers in the victim's throat, but I don't think it will be anything more than from the bedding."

"Okay, Elle, what do you have for us?"

She moved to stand up, but Cat waved her back down. "You don't have to stand."

"Fine by me. I haven't had a chance for all the lab results to be returned, of course, but unless I find something odd, I think it will be the same as the other three. Asphyxiation. Definite recent sex. He is a bit older than the other three."

"By how much?"

"The others were all in their thirties. Anderson was in his late forties."

"Might not matter. There has to be something else that these men did that made them a target," Cat said, working through the issue in her head. "And we don't know for sure if the guys were all heterosexual."

"They handle gay dating too?" Del asked.

"From what I found, yes," Charity said. "The information from HPD wasn't *that* extensive, but we need to check it out further. There is a possibility someone pissed off one of the guys."

"I can look that up," Emma offered.

"No hacking," Del ordered.

"Hacking has a negative connotation to it."

"Because it's illegal," Del shook his head.

His wife snorted. "Too many bloody rules, if you ask me."

"Charity, you can dig around a little more in their site, right?" Cat asked.

Charity nodded. "I'm going to test his blood, but there was little evidence for me to play with, but I can do some more digging around. Oh, and I did get his stomach contents tested. He had some kind of grilled fish and veggies from the looks of it. And less than an hour before he was killed. Nothing on the CCTV, but it's early days."

"I can help," Emma offered.

"No hacking."

"Bloody hell, I just agreed to that. But it will help if two of us are looking. Different perspectives."

"Adam, can you talk to Rome and see if he's heard anything else about these men, and about their cases? I know that the HPD sent over the files on three other murders, but there's always something they leave out."

"Sure thing."

"Anything else?"

Everyone shook their heads. "Good. I'm going to get hold of this Alice Collins and see what she says about these men."

"Be subtle," Del said.

"I'm always subtle."

Cat noticed a woman who paused at the door to their conference room and then came in. She was tall, probably over five nine, and had auburn-colored hair. "Can I help you?"

She smiled. "My name is Autumn Bradford. I'm looking for Martin Delano."

Del stood up. "Ah, yes. Sorry. We were just wrapping up a meeting."

"No worries. I'm a little early. I'm always early, in fact."

"Why don't you follow me into my office?"

No one said anything as they watched the pair of them go into his office. Del got a look at all of them staring at him, so after shutting the door, he shut the blinds as well.

"That was rude," Graeme said, as Marcus walked into the conference room.

"Hey, sorry. I just got finished up with a meeting at Hickam/Pearl Harbor. Did I miss much?"

"I'll go over it with you when we go back out," Adam said.

"Cool. What are we looking at?"

"Del is in the office with a DEA agent" Adam said.

"Former," Emma said.

"I thought you said you didn't remember what he talked about last night?" Adam asked.

"I remember some of it, but I recognize the face." Emma had a photographic memory. Once she saw something, she could not forget it. *Ever.*

"Where from?" Drew asked.

"She was part of a documentary I was watching about that Joyous Wave cult that was on Hawai'i in the nineties. She was in the background of one of the pictures."

Cat blinked. "Does the boss know that?"

"Not sure, but knowing my husband, he does know. You know how he is. Plus, she was in the DEA. They had to have a file on her."

"Well, that's...odd," Elle said.

"But think about it, love. A former cult member is what we were missing in this group."

Drew snorted.

"When do you want to leave to go over to Premiere Connections?" Graeme asked.

"Give me a second. I need to make a call or two and then we can head over."

"Are you going to let Ms. Collins know we're coming?"

"No. I think she's expecting someone, but probably not us. Might give her a little shakeup, and we can get more info out of her."

"Good."

She started off, but Charity came running up behind her. Cat stopped and waited for her to catch up. She couldn't walk that well in heels, but Charity could probably run a 5K.

"Hey, I'm going to start on those security cameras, but I thought you might want to contact some of the folks around there. A lot of rich folks have security cameras around their houses."

"Gotcha. Hey, Adam, do you think you can ask some

of those neighbors around Anderson's house if they have cameras?"

"Sure. I did notice there were two, but they were on rentals, so I have to get hold of the owners for release of the footage."

She nodded. "Let me know if we need to get a search warrant."

As she turned to head back to her office, she caught a glimpse of Drew, who seemed to be following her every move. She rolled her shoulders and continued walking. She couldn't let her growing obsession with him get in her way. She had to get this right. Drew was a distraction that just wouldn't be good for her, and definitely not for him.

She left the files on her desk and grabbed her keys. Time to meet the very rich Alice Collins and get this investigation going.

Del stared across the desk at the women he was sure would be the next TFH member. She was tall for woman, close to six feet. Green eyes sparkled with interest as she took in his office. It was easy to see that she was a local. She dressed in a pair of khaki pants and a blouse. A pair of boots completed the outfit. Her long auburn hair was up in a ponytail, and she wore scant makeup.

"So, you worked for the DEA for ten years?"

"Yes. Right out of college."

"And, since then?"

She shrugged. "I just wanted to take a year off and travel."

He shifted in his seat as he tried to get a handle on the woman. "Just took off?"

"Yeah. I saved up a little money, and I wanted to see more of the world. No ties, so I didn't have to worry about that."

He couldn't even imagine just picking up and leaving.

Even when he had been in his twenties, duty to country always came first. Now, it was his job as the commander of TFH and as a husband and father that kept him tethered to reality.

"The question I have for you is if you disappeared then, how can I be sure that you won't disappear on me?"

"I didn't disappear. I finished up all my cases, gave six months' notice, and flew back at my own expense to testify."

"Yeah, your bosses would hire you back in an instant."

She made a face. "Yeah, no. I wanted to move back to Hawaii. They wanted me on the mainland and saw me as D.C. material."

"And you didn't?"

"I could do the job, but I would hate it. I would rather stab myself in the eyelids with a thousand hot knives than deal with D.C. crap. Plus, they have winter there. I can stand it for a day or two. That's it."

He chuckled. "Yeah, I can see that. I think we need to address your past."

"Ah."

"Yes, ah. You were part of the Joyous Wave cult back in the nineties?"

"It wasn't like I started it. I was only a kid."

"Yes. And you escaped."

"Correct, right before the FBI showed up. That's when they arrested my father."

He blinked. "Your father?"

"Joseph. He was my father. And, not like the other kids, he was my real father. He and my mother founded the cult, although, she got kind of tired of it."

"Yeah?"

"Yeah. He was the typical guy in charge of a cult. Lots of rumors about him sleeping with other women. Mom just disappeared one day. Since she never came forward afterward, I have always wondered if she actually left or if he killed her. We'll never know."

He nodded and thought about the pictures he had seen of her. Her file had been full of them. She had been found by a local boy. Skin and bones and dehydrated and near death. But she had made it out. Due to her tenacity, she had survived and, thanks to her, the federal government had conducted a raid that ended the cult. It was something her bosses at the DEA said about her. The woman just did not give up. On anything.

"Afterwards you lived with your aunt?"

"No. I lived with a woman I called auntie, but she was my foster mother. I didn't have any other family. At least any they could find. But that was probably for the best, considering my parents. Bad blood, if you get my drift?"

"But doesn't that make you tainted?"

She studied him for a long minute, then she laughed. "Yeah, and I *am* a little crazy. I'm sure Donaldson told you that."

Yeah, her last supervisor did mention she had a few screws loose. She often would take some chances that left her in jeopardy, but she always did it to save someone else.

"Can you tell me about the job?" she asked.

"You would work for me, but you would be the liaison for the other law enforcement entities here in Hawaii. You will oversee any of our drug cases; plus, I'll expect you to work cases dealing with other crimes as well."

"Oh, cool. Like the serial killer you're working right now?"

He paused. "Where did you hear about that?"

"I saw your screen when I walked in. Four dead men, all connected in some way." She shrugged. "Serial."

"Your last supervisor said you were too smart for your own good."

"Probably. But, then, if I hadn't been smarter than my father, I'd probably be dead."

He didn't say anything. It was hard to hear someone talk so casually about their father killing them, or saying their mother might be dead.

"Oh, I see you have reservations about my feelings on death. I would never wish anyone dead. Still don't. And I'm sure you read my file like you said. I know I take risks, but I do it to save other people. You will never understand my childhood, or how it warped my view on my parents. They weren't parents. *Ever.* I would have probably had a better childhood if they had left me out in a field to fend for myself as a newborn. "

"Okay, answer me this: why is it so important to save people?"

"I spent my childhood being a victim. I had no choice. I know what it feels like to be lost to the world. That feeling of waking up every day without hope of a better life. It drains your soul. I will do anything to save anyone from the same fate."

He studied her for a long moment. There was no doubting the conviction in her voice. She might be a little different, but they seemed to specialize in that at TFH.

He smiled. "I have a feeling you're going to fit in just fine."

"I got the job?"

He nodded. "Yeah."

"Fantastic."

"I'm sure you'll want to meet the team, but they've probably headed out already."

"No problem."

"But, if you can make it here before eight tomorrow, you can sit in on the morning meeting, and then we can go over and have you fill out all the paperwork. Make sure to bring a copy of your driver's license with you so we can make a copy."

"You got it."

"Let's see if anyone is still around."

He waited for her to stand, then opened the door. Emma was the only one sitting in the conference room.

"Hey," she said smiling at him. "I was just waiting around until you got done. Then I'm gonna help Charity."

36

"No hacking."

She frowned, and he knew she would try her best to resist. Having a wife who was considered one of the best hackers in the Pacific wasn't the easiest thing for him.

"Emma, I would like you to meet Autumn Bradford. Autumn, my wife, Emma, and one of our contractors."

Emma stood. "Nice to meet you. I take it you're hiring her?"

"Emma."

"Emma Thompson?"

She smiled. "Yes." She looked at Del. "See, people know me."

He chuckled. "Yeah, I know."

"You worked with the DEA on that cartel job three years ago. You hacked right into their computers without a problem. We'd been working on that for six months."

"Yeah, kind of sad in my opinion. You'd think the government would have a better group of people working for them."

"I guess I'll get on my way. I just moved in last week, so I am still unpacking. Nice to meet you. And thank you, Del."

"No problem. See you tomorrow."

He stood next to Emma and watched Autumn leave. Once they were alone, he asked, "So, you worked with the DEA?"

She shrugged. "One job. I hate people who sell drugs."

He shook his head. "Why don't I walk you down to see Charity?"

"Sounds like a plan. I think I'm going to like Autumn."

"How do you know that?"

"I just know."

A year ago, his wife couldn't stand meeting new people. The fact that she even talked to Autumn was a big step for her.

"Okay. Either way, it's good to have someone with her knowledge on the team."

His phone buzzed. He pulled it out and almost groaned. The mayor.

"Take it," Emma said as she rose to her tiptoes, and kissed his mouth. "Come get me when you're ready to go home."

"Okay."

He watched as she walked down the hall. Once she was gone, he clicked on the phone.

"Yes, Mr. Mayor."

As the major rambled on about getting updates on the Anderson case, he walked back to his office, his mind already on going home.

"Delano, we have an issue."

"What issue would that be, sir?"

"The FBI is making noises. Apparently, they want to take over the case."

Dammit. Figured.

"Because it's a serial?"

"And the people involved. Lots of money there."

"Great."

"We need to brainstorm. You all know how to catch a serial, so we don't need them for that. We need some reason to keep it in our hands."

Del sat down behind his desk, realizing that getting out of there early wasn't going to happen today.

"All right, tell me what you're thinking."

.

# CHAPTER FOUR

Cat opened the door to Premiere Connections, and held it open for Graeme. The over-chilled air hit her first, causing her to shiver. You can always tell someone was a *haole*, by how cold they kept it inside their homes or office. The next thing that hit was a wave of overpowering floral scents. It was so strong, she almost gagged on it.

"Bloody hell," Graeme muttered.

"Yeah, I feel ya. God, it almost makes me want to throw up."

"Hello, may I help you?"

Cat turned in the direction of the voice. A tall redhead was smiling at them. Lord. She felt puny compared to the woman.

"Hello. I'm Cat Kalakau from Task Force Hawaii. This is Graeme McGregor. We're here to talk to you about Branson Anderson."

She blinked. "I'm not sure I can help you."

"We need to talk to Alice Collins. I hear she's the one in charge," Cat said.

"Uh, yes, but she's in with a client right now. If you

could make an appointment, that would probably work better."

Cat glanced around the waiting room. A handful of clients sat there wearing clothes that probably cost more than a month's pay for her. Then she turned back to the receptionist.

"We need to talk to her right now."

"I am very sorry, but our clients book weeks in advance. There is just no way to fit you in."

Seriously? Why do rich people, and the people who worked for them, think they could schedule time with the police? It's as if being a suspect in any crime was like making a lunch date to them. She shared a look with Graeme, who smiled and nodded.

"Sure. We'll just wait. Not like one of your clients was found murdered this morning after having a date with someone in your agency or anything. No rush."

"Is that true?" a youngish Asian man asked her.

"No," the receptionist blurted out.

"Yes," Cat said almost at the same time.

She gave the woman a large smile.

"Fine. Come on," she muttered.

She heard Graeme chuckle behind her as they followed the woman through the door, then down a long hallway. She could hear faint voices on the other sides of the closed doors. It sounded like there were a lot of clients being interviewed.

"Wait in here please. I will get Ms. Collins to speak with you."

They stepped into the room. Cat was a little bit taken aback by the luxury. It was all plush and shiny, something that probably appealed to one percenters. The walls were a soft blue. Against the back wall of the room was an overstuffed, rather large couch. In front of it was a table that had some glasses and a pitcher filled with cucumber water.

"Bloody hell."

"Again, you said a mouthful," Cat said walking forward.

"Why does a person need something like this?"

"It's not that easy meeting people."

She poured herself some water. She loved cucumber water. It was one of the very few things her mother and she agreed upon.

"What's hard about it? See someone, go up and ask them out."

She had just taken a sip of water, and she started to choke on it. Graeme smacked her on her back a few times hard enough to bruise.

"Are you okay?"

"Yes," she said, coughing. "It's just you giving dating advice."

"What? I know how to date. Didn't I catch the prettiest woman on the island?"

She smiled at him. The courtship of Graeme and Elle had not been easy for either one of them, but it was so wonderful to see them happy.

"Yes. Yes, you did."

There was a quick knock, then the door opened. "Oh, hello. Sorry it took me so long to get down here," the woman said. She was another tall one with blond hair and bright blue green eyes. She looked just like her picture, but even better. Only someone evil looked better than their photo shopped pic.

"I'm Cat Kalakau and this is Graeme McGregor with TFH. We're here about Branson Anderson."

"Yes, Tiffany told me. Please sit down."

Collins waited until they sat on the couch, and she took a chair facing them.

"It is just horrible. Branson was a really great guy."

"Can you tell us how long he has been a member of your client list?"

She hesitated. "We have strict confidentiality clauses about that."

41

"Anderson is dead. He doesn't care," Graeme said.

Cat had to suppress a laugh. Graeme was blunt, but sometimes it worked. "And we can get a warrant. We are already working on that, and we will file if needed. If you would rather keep it out of court—meaning public record— I would suggest that you give us the information."

"Well…"

"If it becomes public, your client list might just dwindle."

She should feel guilty about pressing the woman, but this was murder. Four in fact. And while Del had told her to be subtle, there was subtle for regular people—and there was subtle for the TFH.

Collins sighed. "Okay. Yes, Branson was one of our clients."

"Older than your normal client?"

"Not really. We have all age groups, but we have begun working with divorced men, those looking to start out on the second phase of their lives."

Meaning, when they divorced their first wife, they were looking for a trophy wife.

"And Branson was that?"

"Yes. He had lost his wife about five years ago. Cancer. He hadn't really dated anyone seriously since then. He wanted to date women who were looking for more than a good time."

"And how many different women did he date?" Cat asked.

"Three, I believe."

"Their names?"

Alice hesitated.

Cat sighed. "Really? You're going to hold back again?"

She straightened her shoulders and her eyes sparked with more than a little irritation. This was the businesswoman who had developed a successful company. Not only that, she did it with a limited pool of customers.

Cat knew that she would be smart to remind herself this wasn't a stupid woman.

"I promise my clients complete confidentiality."

"Do you also promise they'll survive their dates?"

She glanced back and forth between her and Graeme. "What are you saying?"

"I have a feeling that if it got out you had a killer targeting your clients, it would deter people from using your services."

There was a beat of silence as Alice continued to stare at Cat. Apparently, she was used to intimidating women, but Cat worked with men. She had no problem doing a stare down.

"Are you threatening me?"

"I'm just saying that we already have the press sniffing around for information about the case. If we can't get those names from you, we'll have to get a warrant. That will become public information."

She sat back in her chair, an air of irritation surrounding her. She didn't like what was happening.

"I will have to talk to my lawyer. I would rather keep this out of the public, but I also have to protect myself."

"You make sure you call me by tomorrow morning," Cat said, standing and pulling out her card. She handed it to Alice. "If you don't, I'll talk to a judge."

"Understood."

"We'll see ourselves out," Cat said.

She didn't think to look behind her to make sure that Graeme was following. She knew he was there. Once they were outside, Graeme whistled.

"That was one cool customer. She's not liking you at the moment."

Cat shrugged. "Those types rarely do."

"What's that mean?"

"She was probably a former cheerleader, expects everyone to fall all over themselves to make her happy. You notice she kept smiling until I pressed her on stuff.

And when she realized I was in charge."

"And she just met a woman who doesn't give a damn."

She laughed. "You got that right. Let's head back. I have some calls to make, and I know you want to check on Elle."

"She thinks I worry too much."

They reached the SUV and she looked at him. "She does, but I know it's comforting. Take it from me, it's a lot better to have someone be a little bit over the top with their worrying. As I said, it's comforting to her."

"Hey, do you mind stopping off at Ala Moana? Elle likes the edamame shakes there."

"Good, because I can pick something up. I'm starving."

\* \* \*

Adam pulled off Kalanianaole Highway to hit up the friend of the first victim. He had just finished going over everything with Marcus, who seemed to have his mind on something else. Of course, since he had to deal with the military and terrorism, it was probably work.

"So, this new woman…we're expanding?" Marcus asked.

"Yeah. Which means they are going to be throwing more work our way."

Marcus grunted.

"It also means you'll have more time for all those terrorism task forces they keep putting you on. Del made noises about sending you to some conferences."

"Oh, good God, why? I hate those damned things"

Adam chuckled. "Del thinks we need to have more contacts. He doesn't always trust the military to be forthcoming with information because they see us as civilians."

"He was special forces."

"Yeah, so that means he knows."

Adam pulled up to the driveway and hit the speaker box.

"Yes?" a male voice said.

"Hello, my name is Adam Lee from Task Force Hawaii. I'm here to see Michael Cheng."

"Yes, of course. I'll buzz you in."

The gate slowly opened, and Adam drove his SUV up to the house.

"These rich folks live in Hawaii, but do everything they can not to experience Hawaii," Marcus said, shaking his head.

"Bruddah, you said a mouthful."

Once Adam parked his vehicle, they walked up to the front door. It opened before they reached it. A small Asian man smiled at them. Dressed in khaki shorts and a blue Hawaiian shirt, he looked to be in his early forties.

"Hello, I'm Adam Lee and this is Marcus Floyd," Adam said, showing the man his badge. The other man gave it a cursory look, then waved them in. "Come in."

They followed him into the house. Both he and Marcus removed their shoes, then walked down the hall behind the man. The house was nice enough, but it was filled with so many golden figurines and embellishments, that it almost overwhelmed the small hallway.

Mr. Cheng led them out onto a lanai that overlooked a pool and further on, the beach.

"Damn," Marcus muttered just loud enough for Adam to hear.

"Please, come sit. It's a nice morning out."

Once they were seated, Adam retrieved his notepad. "Now, you were a good friend of Sam Waters?"

He nodded. "Yeah, I was his godfather actually. After his parents passed, I helped him start up his business."

"And he was a DJ?"

"Yeah, one of the hottest on the islands. He had even gotten a few gigs over on the mainland. He was also talking about moving over there."

"We wanted to ask you if there was anything that you remember from the weeks leading up to his death?"

He shook his head. "Not really."

"He was using Premiere Connections, is that right?" Adam asked.

Mr. Cheng made a face. "He did for a few months, but then he stopped, oh about a week or two before his death. He was convinced it was a waste of time."

"Why do you say that?" Marcus asked.

"Not sure. He did say he was fed up with the dates. They never seemed to go anywhere, and they always wanted to go out on his dime. Sam had a lot of money, and he didn't mind spending it. But not one of those dates ever wanted to hang out at the beach or just take a nice drive. They always wanted him to spend, spend, spend."

"Was that the only reason he was fed up?" Marcus asked.

Mr. Cheng shook his head. "No. The last few weeks before his death, he said he'd been getting some odd letters."

"Letters?" Adam asked.

"Yeah, weird things. I thought it was odd they were coming in the mail. Kids his age are all texts or emails. Not with this woman though."

"Did he say it was one of his dates?"

"No. I don't know if he knew, but it was enough to stop him from using the service. In fact, about three days before he was murdered, he got a dozen roses delivered to one of the clubs where he was working. I think that freaked him out a little bit."

"Did he say who they were from?" Adam asked, notating the dates down in his notebook.

Cheng shook his head. "Again, I don't think he knew. Nothing else came, no more letters or flowers. Then, he was dead. I didn't think to mention it when I talked to the police originally. It didn't seem that important at the time."

"No worries, Mr. Cheng," Adam said as he shared a look with Marcus.

After a few more minutes of questioning, Adam and

Marcus left Mr. Cheng with the promise they would let him know if anything turned up.

"So, what do you think?" Marcus asked. "It's undoubtedly the first lead outside of Premiere Connections anyone has gotten in the case."

Adam nodded. "We need to get hold of everyone else."

"Okay, we have Charlie Xan. Does he have any family here?"

He shook his head. "They are living on the mainland now. I think after his murder, they just left. I have their number though. Then there's the other guy. But his entire family lives on the mainland. Cat's going to talk to Anderson's sons as soon as they get in."

"Let me guess, they live on the mainland?"

"No. I think they were over there for business, but she's going to talk to them. Now that we have this info, we can see if their father had any issues before his death."

"So, we possibly have a female stalker trolling Premiere Connections for her next victim?"

"Or it could be a guy. Could be a man who is so damned jealous of what is going on, that he stalks the male clients. Who knows?"

"At least we have a lead."

"Finally."

"Great, now, it's my turn to pick the music."

Adam groaned as Marcus turned the station from Island 98.5 to the country channel. It was an agreement they'd made earlier this year. Adam hated country music and Marcus hated Hawaiian music. Their split time of radio control had been the only thing that had kept them from arguing. There was a commercial and then some song came on. Twangy guitars filled the SUV.

"You weren't raised right, man," Adam said.

"If you can't appreciate The Zac Brown band, you just don't know good music."

Adam rolled his eyes, and pulled onto the highway that lead back to the office. He could handle it, at least for the next thirty minutes.

Drew stepped off the elevator in the basement to head to Charity's lab when his cell went off. The ominous sounds of Beethoven's Fifth told him that it was his mother.

"Hello, Mom."

"Hello to you. What are you doing?"

"I'm working."

"Yes, but what are you doing today at work?"

He rolled his eyes as he pulled open the door to the lab. Charity smiled at him then cocked her head. He mouthed the word *mother* and Charity laughed.

"You know I can't tell you about any ongoing investigations."

"I didn't want you to tell me anything that was classified."

"I don't have classified information, Mom. It's just not out to the public yet."

"I heard a few customers mention the Branson Anderson murder today."

And she knew that TFH probably got the case. They were handed all the high-profile murders like this, and Anderson being the victim made it high profile. His mother was an invariable gossip. More than likely, she had customers asking her about it. Every regular who dined at their restaurants knew about his job. And if they didn't, his mother told them. It was annoying and embarrassing just how proud she was of him.

"As I said, you know I can't talk about an ongoing investigation. Besides, we don't know much at this point."

There was a beat of silence. "Okay. But since you can't help me with that, why don't you come to dinner this weekend?"

He closed his eyes and shook his head. This was not a

good sign. Since the shooting, his mother had stopped trying to set him up. Before, it had been horrible. Every able-bodied woman she deemed good enough for her son got pulled into an uncomfortable situation where his mother threw not so subtle hints throughout dinner. Worse, she'd used guilt to get him to attend. And he did, even knowing what was going to happen. In the last nine months, he had been given a reprieve, but apparently, Rose Franklin was done waiting.

"Like you said, we have a new case and I might be too busy."

Another pause, and not a good sign. "Okay. But keep it in mind."

He blinked, surprised by her easy acceptance. "Of course. Bye, mom."

He hung up and looked at Charity, who was shaking her head.

"What were you lying about?"

"I wasn't lying. I said that maybe I would be busy."

She studied him as if he were one of the specimens sent up from the morgue. They had a sibling-like relationship, one that definitely gave them both the right to speak their minds.

"I'm just saying that I don't want to be standing near you during a lightning storm. And if she asks me about it next time I see her, I'll have to tell her the truth."

"You are a traitor and I disown you. She's up to something. I know it."

"You act like she's conspiring against you."

Drew shook his head. "You have no idea. She could outmaneuver any general."

She shook her head, then turned back to her computer. "What are you doing down here?"

"I came to see if you'd made any progress."

"I always make progress, but on the case, one thing. HPD sent the files from the other three cases. We had some of it, but not the nitty gritty. I don't know how they expected me to really know whether the cases were connected by the crappy files they sent over."

He could tell from the gleam in Charity's eye, she was ready to go on a rant. Usually, Drew enjoyed them, but for some reason, he wasn't in the mood.

"But you found something, because you are the queen of forensics."

She studied him, then smiled. "You know that's right. I found similar fibers. Red silk, like a scarf or something."

"Definitely linked?"

"Possibly, which is asinine on their part, because they should have already declared it a serial."

"That's odd."

"It is, because it isn't like them to let something like this slip. They have a good crew over there."

"So, they're connected?"

"As I said, possibly."

"Possibly. I know that Del was upset that the FBI was trying to come and take over the case."

"Yeah, I heard about that. I think they ironed it out though. And now, I'm stuck here looking at these," she said motioning toward the monitor. "Emma had to get home. The babysitter had some kind of emergency."

"I can help."

"Are you sure?"

"We have nothing else to do, and Elle already went home. Still, there's nothing to do unless we get called out."

"Good deal."

She set him up on another computer.

"Now, what are we looking for?" he asked as he brought up one of the CCTV recordings.

"Anything out of place. Someone driving erratically."

They sat in silence as they looked over the video. "None of this is going to be conclusive."

"I know, but it might give us a lead. Then that could lead us to at least a suspect."

He nodded. "I always thought it was interesting that

there were no cameras throughout Waimanalo and Kailua."

She shrugged. "They don't have them for Kam Highway and part of H-2 either. I'm sure it has something to do with the weather. Plus, there aren't a lot of traffic signals there."

"You know, there are a few convenience stores in that area. There has to be at least one that has some kind of security cameras."

"Yeah, I checked and they are sending over the video. Our main problem is many of those places only hold them over for twenty-four hours, then record over existing footage. But we might find something."

"That's good."

"How are you doing?"

"What do you mean?" he asked, without looking over at her.

"Don't make me hit you."

She shook her head. "I'm fine. It isn't like it's a big deal."

She didn't say anything else, but he could feel her gaze on him.

He glanced over. "What?"

"It *is* a big deal. Neither of you have dealt with the issue at hand."

He rolled his eyes. "Good lord, we have. We weren't made for each other."

"How do you know that?"

He hated when charity got chatty like this. It was annoying, and it made him think about his failed relationship with Cat.

"I thought you were still pissed at her."

"Not really."

"And, I know we aren't for each other because she told me."

"She said that?"

"Yes. Well, sort of. She told me she wasn't made for a

relationship. I'm not made for a woman who can't even think of that possibility. I don't expect marriage, or even living together, but if a woman can't even fathom something serious with me after knowing me so long, I really don't want to waste my time."

She looked like she wanted to argue. If there was something that Charity was better at other than forensics, it was arguing. But, thankfully, she decided not to.

"How about we get this done and you come with me and TJ to dinner? We're going to hit Honolulu Sushi for dinner."

His first inclination was to say no. But, he had been spending too much time at home, and he hadn't seen TJ since he had gotten back from the mainland.

"Sounds like a date."

And maybe he could convince his mother that was exactly what it had been.

"All right, let's get this done so we can meet him there," Charity said with a smile.

He decided if they hurried, he might just avoid running into Cat again today. He could lie to Charity all he wanted, but there was no denying that when he had to be in the same room as Cat, he couldn't think straight.

Maybe one day, he would learn to take her advice and forget they ever had a date, or a moment. But until then, he was doomed to suffer.

# CHAPTER FIVE

The next morning, Cat felt as if her ass was dragging across the floor. She'd had little-to-no-sleep because she'd been busy looking over the case files. Usually, it wasn't that hard to do, but having three different detectives on the three different murders made it difficult. Each detective had their own style, and it took some time to get accustomed to it. Which meant that she had to reread reports over and over to get at their meanings. She could contact all three of them, but cops sometimes became overly sensitive when another law enforcement organization started to review their work. Even if they had done no wrong, they would assume the worst.

On top of that, the entire case was about to explode publically. People were already linking the other killings with this one and, after that, the tweets started to flow in. It would only take a few hours before the whole thing became a madhouse. It's why she decided to have another organizational meeting that morning. She'd texted everyone early to let them know they needed to go over the evidence. It wasn't something they always did, but she felt it was important. Del had agreed, from the text he sent back.

Her phone vibrated to tell her she had a text. She pulled it out of her pocket, and almost groaned aloud when she saw her mother's face. She had avoided talking to family last night. There was some drama going on with her youngest sister, but there was always something going on with her youngest sister. If Cat stopped work every time her mother called about Marie, Cat would never get anything done.

If you do not text back, I will assume you are dead and call the police.

Her mother was completely ignoring the fact that Cat was an actual policewoman. It was her mother's way of reminding Cat she didn't like what she did for a living.

Cat had her head down as she pushed through the front door to the office. She walked into a solid wall of muscle. She dropped her phone and bit back a gasp as she looked up.

"Hey, careful," Drew said.

It wasn't his normal every day voice she was used to. It was the one she'd heard that night, the one that had tried to tempt her back to his room. Then she realized something else. Drew had muscles. Lots of them. He had always been kind of lean, but lately, Cat knew he had been working out. Charity had let it slip that her boyfriend, TJ, had been training Drew. It'd been easy to see he was busting out of some of his t-shirts, and the last six months had left him pretty bulked up. While she pretended to ignore Drew, Cat always had her ears open to hear about what he might be doing. Because she was pathetic like that.

"Sorry," she mumbled, leaning down to pick up her phone.

As she rose up, she found him standing in the same spot. He was staring at her with the same expression that always made her lose most rational thought. It hadn't always been that way. Now, though, she knew what lay behind that expression. After their first kiss, she understood the intense passion hidden beneath his cool surface.

"When's the meeting this morning?"

Meeting? What meeting? Oh, right, work. That was all they talked about these days. "At the top of the hour."

"Great. I need some coffee. I should be back in time."

She said nothing, because she was still trying to get her mind to return to the conversation and not on the need to lean closer and touch…or lick. She could smell the ocean air on him; mixed with the deep, masculine scent that called to her. Still. She wanted to get closer, feel his hands on her flesh again.

"Are you okay, Cat?"

She blinked, bringing herself to the present from that side trip to her favorite fantasy. "Uh, yeah. Sorry. I was up late working."

"Okay. Be back in a few."

Then he was gone. She stood there for a second and tried her best to get her heartbeat under control. Heat crackled through her, and she wanted nothing more than to run after him just so she could be near him. It was always like this, and it was only getting worse. They had avoided each other easily before, but with her in charge of the case, it was going to be hard to do now.

"Hey, Cat," Del said as he walked over toward her.

"Morning, boss."

"You look tired. Don't let this case get to you."

"I was just trying to catch up."

"Good deal. I hear that Adam got some info for the meeting. He talked to a few of the victim's friends, and he's found a common thread."

"Great."

His cell rang and he pulled it out. The puzzled look on his face did not bode well. "Yes?"

Someone talked very rapidly on the other end of the line.

"Why, yes, I know your daughter, and she's standing right here in front of me. No reason to call the *real* police."

Oh, God, she was going to kill her mother. No jury would convict her with this kind of evidence, she was sure of it. Of all the embarrassing things her mother could do, this was right at the top of the list.

"No worries, Ms. Kalakau. Cat is busy with a big case. You can blame me for that."

He listened for a second, then, "Yes, I understand family is important, but this is Cat's first case as lead investigator. We're all pretty proud of her."

Great, now he sounded like her kindergarten teacher. Her mother always reduced people to trying to satisfy her every whim. It was one of the reasons Cat had moved out. She loved her mother, but she was a tiny little dictator who knew exactly how to turn the enemy into her puppets.

She motioned for Del to give her the phone, which he did.

"Here's Cat. It was very nice talking to you."

He handed her the phone. "Come to my office when you're done. I want to talk to you about an idea I have."

She nodded and took the phone. "Mom. You should *never* call my boss."

"You didn't answer. I thought you were dead."

"Really? Because you don't sound too sad about it."

"I know you're alive now. Before, I was panicked."

More than likely irritated. "Is there something you needed?"

"It's Marie."

"Mom, it's always Marie," she said as she started walking toward Del's office.

"She wants to get married."

Cat stopped in her tracks. "What?"

"Your sister wants to marry that boy."

She sighed. "Marie is twenty-two. Her boyfriend is twenty-five. You can't stop them. They are old enough to make their own decisions and live with the consequences."

There was a pause from her mother. "So, you will not help?"

"I'll call her when I get a chance and talk to her. But I'm not going to talk her out of it."

"Fine."

"I have a meeting with the boss. And, I am leading a meeting later. I really have to go."

"Call me later."

"If I get a chance, I will. Bye, mom."

"Bye."

She didn't give her mother a chance to say anything else. She clicked off Del's phone and made her way to his office. She knocked on the doorjamb and he looked up from his desk.

"Sorry," she said as she walked into his office and handed him his phone.

"No worries. Moms are kind of a pain. Mine wants daily updates on the baby."

Del's mom lived on the mainland, and didn't get to see her granddaughter as much as she wanted. She knew it had to be hard to live that far away from family. Still, there was a part of her that would like to try it at least for a little while. It would be amazing not to be hounded by her mother every day. But, there was a good chance her mother wouldn't let the Pacific Ocean slow her down.

"Shut the door and sit down."

His jovial manner had disappeared, and now he was all business. One day into her investigation, this did not bode well for her. Her nerves immediately jumped. She did as he asked, wondering what this was all about.

"I'm getting some pushback on the search warrant."

"For PC rolls? We don't even want all of them. Just the names of the women who dated the four men."

"I know. And we'll get them, but I've been thinking. What do you think is the best way to talk to these women who dated the victims?"

"I planned on finding the same women they all dated and then eliminating from there."

"And how would do you do that?"

"We would have to interview them. I was going to talk to you about how to do that. Pulling them in would make it more efficient, but it would also set their alarms off. It might be better to approach them at home or work, catch them off guard."

He nodded. "That was my thought too. There can't be that many women who dated all four men."

"But?"

"I think I might have a better plan. Or a plan that we could run outside of the main investigation."

"Yeah?"

"If we go at them head on, we'll spook them, but I thought if we could get someone undercover, that might work too."

"Undercover? I think that might be difficult. We would have to have a great backfill on the person."

"That was exactly what I was thinking. We need someone who fits the bill of the clientele and who already has a connection with TFH."

Something itched between her shoulder blades. Before he said the name, she knew who it was going to be.

"Drew."

"Yeah. And let me tell you why."

Drew returned just in time for the meeting. He jogged up the stairs, and hurried into the conference room. He didn't want everyone to think he was doing this to avoid Cat. He wasn't. He had just needed a break. It was bad enough that he had to sit through an entire meeting where she was front and center, but the simple byplay this morning still had his body humming.

It wasn't that difficult to understand why. The moment she had collided with him, he had bit back his need to touch. He had a feeling he would be able to detect that herbal soap scent from her on his clothes, but he thought people would think him strange if he walked around smelling his shirt.

Everyone was already seated at the table, but there was one seat left for him. He slipped into the chair beside Charity, who looked at his cup of coffee with a frown.

"You didn't get me one?"

"Tell the FBI agent to get you one."

She chuckled as Del stood up. Cat stood off to his right in the background, and she didn't look happy. He had been worried when he saw her earlier. She looked tired, almost worn out. Work was her focus, and with this case, he knew she would be stressed out. He hoped that nothing bad had happened since the day before, but sometimes that was the way their cases went. TFH got a lot of unsolved cases where the crimes either had national security implications, or they had a criminal who was ramping up the violence.

"Before we get started, I wanted to introduce Autumn Bradford," Del said. "She's joining the team after a pretty damned spectacular career with the DEA. She's originally from the islands, so she knows her way around."

Drew looked at the woman seated at the end of the table. Long auburn-colored hair, green eyes, and a sweet smile. It didn't hide the mischievous expression. He had a feeling the woman used the smile to get what she wanted. Not in a bad way, but he was sure many people would look at her and think she was just a little sweet thing with no brain. Del wouldn't have hired her if that were the case.

"Aloha," she said to the table in general, but her attention seemed to snag on him before moving on.

"Ho, looks like the new girl is interested in you, Drew," Charity whispered.

He just shook his head and sipped his coffee, although, he did notice she glanced at him one more time before looking at Del again.

"Oh, yeah, she's interested in you, my man."

"Cut it out," he whispered under his breath.

"She's going to get settled in; plus, she has all the paperwork that comes with working for the state to work on. But, I thought I would have her sit in today to get a feel of how we work. Cat, you're up."

Del sat back down and Cat stepped up. He tried to prepare himself for the impact but, of course, he failed. She was wearing her signature camo pants, black t-shirt, and boots. She always left him on edge, but after touching her this morning, that edge was jagged. Now he had to sit through a meeting that would have his attention focused solely on her.

She had worn her hair up in a ponytail, and he liked it that way. Every time she moved her head, it swayed behind her. But he liked it down too. He just loved it period.

She started talking and, for a moment, he didn't hear her words. He watched the way her mouth moved.

He could almost remember the way she tasted when he'd kissed her.

Charity nudged him with her elbow, causing him to spill some of his coffee.

"Watch it," he muttered.

"Stop drooling."

He shook himself and gave his friend a dirty look, then turned around to listen to Cat.

"We are going to end up having to get a court order for the women these men dated. We can see why the victims signed up, but the confidentiality clause still holds for linking them up to see who they dated."

"Great," Del said. "I had a feeling, but I thought maybe Graeme would charm it out of the owner."

Elle snorted. "Fat chance there."

"Moving on, I think Adam has some updates he wants to give us."

She took her seat and Adam took over. Drew could finally breathe a sigh of relief—at least for the moment.

"We went to talk to a friend of Sam Waters. His godfather, in fact. After that, we got on the phone to speak to some of the relatives of these other victims. We found out that they were all probably being stalked in the last few weeks leading up to their deaths."

He clicked on the control panel and a screen came up with all four men.

"We don't know about Anderson, but I'm sure Cat will be talking to his relatives again, right?"

She nodded. "Yeah, I spoke to his sons over the phone. They are supposed to try to make it back today or tomorrow."

"We aren't sure if they all received the same kinds of notes," Adam continued. "It's been months since the deaths of the other three, so that information is lost. But, one thing is that shortly before their murders, they all received flowers."

"Flowers? Like delivered to them?" Cat asked.

"Yes. It would be one here and there, then leading up to the killing, it would become one delivery a day. And it didn't matter if they refused."

"Another thread HPD missed," Charity murmured.

"I checked on that. I put a call in to Rome Carino," Del said. He looked at Autumn. "He's our HPD liaison. At first, the three cases weren't connected. Sure, three men were murdered, but the problem was that they were months apart. And worse, three different detectives were involved; so, until some lawmakers started making noise, they didn't connect them."

"Still," Charity said crossing her arms beneath her breasts, then eyeing Drew's coffee.

"Don't even think about it," he muttered under his breath.

"You are a mean, stupid boy," Charity whispered.

"Our best bet is probably going to be talking to Anderson's sons. Their recollection of what was going on right before their father died will be fresher. Plus, children are more involved in their parents' lives than just friends. At least, that's the feeling I got when I talked to them," Cat said.

"The first three murders were several months apart, and it has been six months since this last one," Adam said. "Unless we can narrow down the suspect pool, we are going to be screwed. We'll just have to sit around."

"We'll get a search warrant, but I talked to Del before the meeting and we came up with an idea," Cat said, pausing to let Del take over.

"We need someone on the inside."

"At Premiere Connections?" Graeme asked. "Working for them?"

"Not quite. That would be hard to do, especially with the time constraints. PC does extensive background checks on all their employees. They even do a financial records check," Cat explained.

"I think it has to do with their clients. Lots of money there, and people could take advantage of it," Charity said. "When I worked for the C.I.A., they did that to make sure someone couldn't be bought off. If you have a lot of debt, you are a security risk."

"So," Del said, taking back control of the conversation, "we need someone who can be a client. If we go in there head on and interview them, they will clam up. Even if they aren't guilty. While we handle our investigation on the outside, our insider will go on a few dates," Del said. He shared a look with Cat, who did not look happy. "We need someone who is a local, someone with money. Someone who isn't *really* a cop."

"It would also help if they are well-known and have deep roots in the community," Cat said, her voice flat and almost unemotional. "Also helpful if he'd been in the news lately. That seems to be a theme as well."

There was a long moment of silence, and it seemed the entire table turned and looked at him. He added up all the criteria needed for the undercover client, and realized why they were all staring at him.

"Damn."

# CHAPTER SIX

Drew stared out the window in Del's office. The late afternoon traffic was starting to pick up. Tourists and locals, vying for the best lane to get them to their destinations. Everyone in such a hurry to get to their next stop. He watched them, attempting to get his emotions under control, and failing. He had worked for TFH since its inception, but he had never wanted to work in the field. He wasn't cut out for undercover.

"Drew?" Del asked.

Drew waited for another second or two before he glanced over his shoulder. Del was leaning up against his desk, his arms crossed over his chest. Adam sat in one of the chairs in front of the desk, and of course, there was Cat. She occupied the other chair. She hadn't said anything since they had arrived in Del's office.

"What?"

"What are your thoughts about going undercover?"

He shrugged. "I don't know how to do it, if that's what you mean. I work in the morgue with Elle for a reason. I'm not made for direct investigation. I'm not good at playing make believe."

"No. And you don't need to know how. You're just going to be used to trap the killer. Or, at least sniff out a lead or two. Just be yourself."

"Sure, that's easy," he said, not even trying to hide his sarcasm. "Because it's easier when you're deceiving people."

Adam and Del shared a look.

"I know it won't be easy," Del said. "We'll get the search warrant, but this will allow us to get ahead of the game. We're behind right now. Sifting through all the evidence, not to mention tracking down some more statements from friends and family members, is going to take some time. If we can find out who they dated in common, we can cut down a lot of that time. We need someone to be there on the frontlines."

"So, you want to use me as bait?"

Adam chuckled. "In a way, and it works with your background. You're an island boy and, while you work with us, you aren't listed as an agent or detective. Which means, you can go in as yourself. Your family connections help. You've been in the news too."

"That's a connection?"

Adam shrugged and looked over at Cat, waiting for her to answer. When she didn't, he did.

"All of the victims had some coverage for various things. Of course, all of them worked with charities, or public companies that made a lot of money. That tends to get you in the news a lot, so that might not even be news." He smiled. "Like we said, you just have to be yourself."

He snorted. "Well, that will impress them."

"I want to express my objection to this again," Cat said.

Drew blinked at the venom in her voice. She didn't look at him when she spoke. Instead, she was intently staring at Del. Her whole body vibrated with anger.

"And, I said I understood, but I overruled that. I explained it before," Del stated, with no hint of anger in his tone. "It's your case, but I'm the boss."

"Yes. I just wanted to get it out there for Drew."

"Excuse me?" Damn, he hadn't meant to sound so damned mean. He cleared his throat. "You didn't want me to do this?"

When she said nothing, he looked at Del. Their boss glanced between them. "Cat was worried you were inexperienced."

"Not to mention that we are dealing with a maniac hunting men and killing them," she said.

A year ago, he would have been thrilled with the worry he heard in her voice. Now, he knew that she felt he was weak. She assumed because he wasn't some big bruiser who carried a gun and could kick down doors, that he couldn't handle the job. That just pissed him off. When he was mad, he often made rash decisions, and now was no different.

"I'll do it," he said without breaking eye contact with Cat.

"Are you sure?" Del asked.

He shrugged and glanced at his boss. "If I feel like I can't help after the initial meeting, we can do something else. Right now, this might be the easiest way to work through the women."

"Okay. Well, I think we can set up a meeting tomorrow with Premiere Connections. Graeme said they were busy today, right, Cat?"

Cat sighed. "Yeah, they were, but I have a feeling it wouldn't be that tough to get at least an initial appointment."

"Sounds good," Del said. "I really appreciate you doing this."

Drew nodded. "No worries. I have some things to finish up before I leave tonight, so if there isn't anything else?"

"No, go on."

He left them and headed to the morgue, but found

himself turning in the direction of Charity's lab. When he arrived, he found her watching security camera footage.

"Hey, there, Drew," she said with a smile. "How did it go?"

He shrugged, but didn't answer right away. His stomach was still tied in knots. Now that a few minutes had passed and he was no longer in Cat's presence, he was starting to have second thoughts.

"You look a little out of sorts. I take it you're going to do the job?"

He nodded. "It makes sense. I have the island connections. Plus, all the men involved had been in the news within the last eighteen months of their killings. I fit that bill."

The shooting that almost killed him had been front page news for weeks.

"The news connection is a thing?" she asked.

He shrugged. "Not sure if it is, but they all were."

"Is that what has you upset?"

"No."

She paused the footage and looked at him. "What then?"

He sighed. "Cat didn't want me to do it."

"Did she say why?"

"She felt it was too dangerous for me."

Charity didn't say anything at first, then she asked, "What did she say exactly?"

"She raised an objection and mentioned a maniac killing men." He shrugged. "I don't know what she said privately to Del before the meeting, but apparently, they had words about it."

Charity shook her head. "I think you're reading her wrong."

"What do you mean?"

"I don't think it has to do with that. I think she might have issues with you still."

"What do you mean?"

"I can't say more than that, but just know that her objection has more to do with her feelings *for* you than *about* you."

"What the hell does that mean?"

"I can tell you what it means," Emma said from behind them. She was standing there smiling, holding Evie in her arms.

"Baby!" Charity said and hurried forward. "Hello, darlin'."

Drew shook his head. He still didn't understand the way women went pule over babies

"So, you want me to tell you?" Emma asked.

Emma hadn't been that good with relationships on a personal or professional level before meeting Del. Still, she was a keen observer so, more than likely, her insight would help.

"Sure."

"Cat has feelings for you still. She doesn't want you hurt, and she's a bit protective over you. That's what Charity meant. Plus, working with you might just drive her crazy."

He blinked, trying to gather all his thoughts together. These two women were making no sense.

"We work together now."

"Yeah, but think about it. You're going to be on dates with women and wearing a wire. That is not going to be fun for her."

He rolled his eyes. "Yeah, right."

Charity walked back and forth with the baby, who was fussing a bit. "That's why I didn't say anything. You wouldn't believe me. You have a blind spot when it comes to Cat."

As she neared Drew, Evie leaned toward him. He took the baby easily. In a family the size of his, he was always holding some baby. Of course, Evie settled down immediately.

"The baby whisperer," Charity said with a laugh.

"I hate that name."

The women in the office started calling him that when he had been the only one who could get Evie to calm down when she was just a month old. Now, they all thought he had some kind of magic touch with babies. It just came from being one of many cousins. From the time he could hold a baby, there was usually one in his arms at family gatherings.

"You shouldn't hate it. It's sweet."

"I still don't get it. He doesn't whisper to them."

Emma was ten times better at communications than she had been before getting married, but she sometimes missed things.

"Like the horse whisperer. We explained that, Emma."

"Still." She looked at Drew and smiled. "You are good with babies."

He shook his head and handed Evie over to Emma. "I gotta get going. I have a report to file, then I have a date with Charity's boyfriend."

Charity laughed. "Good thing too. Before you two started working out, he was making noises about weight training with me. I might have dumped him and called off the wedding."

"Call me if you need any help."

He needed to get away and get his head screwed on straight. A night of exercise and male camaraderie would help.

Charity and Emma watched Drew leave.

"That boy is obtuse," Charity said.

Emma snorted. "All men are."

"No, he really thinks that Cat doesn't like him."

"Well, she does. He's just being a man."

Charity shook her head. "I wish he had never been

shot. They might have had a chance."

Emma opened her mouth, then snapped it shut.

"What?"

Charity waited, knowing it was a requirement with Emma. Long silences followed by bursts of energy were her style.

"It might have hurt them, and maybe they will never recover, but maybe it will make them fight harder."

"How?"

She shrugged. "I didn't have it easy, so when I finally found Del, it made me appreciate him more. They have both grown this last year. Drew especially. He displays a confidence he didn't have before. And I'm thankful you finally took him shopping. None of his shirts fit him."

Charity laughed. "He has bulked up, but I get what you mean. You're right, too. I have never seen him so confident. We were out at the beach last weekend, and women were watching his every move. Boy had no idea they were watching him either."

"I think they have a chance."

Charity gave her a side glance.

"How much of one?"

Emma laughed. "I say they don't last a week before they both lose control, so I say after the first 'date' she'll lose it."

"I better text Elle and see if she wants in."

"Just don't tell my husband. Del forbade me to bet on any more of what he called silly wagers. Other than baby wagers. Why the hell that is okay and the others aren't, I don't know."

Charity laughed and started her text. "Does he think he has any control over you?"

"No, but it's a fun game for us to pretend."

The next morning arrived too soon. Drew wasn't in the mood to deal with working with Cat, and he despised computer dating type services. It seemed so damned clinical to him; although, he knew his cousin was happily married to a woman he had met on one of those sites. For Drew, they never seemed to work out.

After filling out the application the night before, he had prepared for today. He might not be part of the *in the field* investigative team, but he knew how to handle this. Adam had talked to him before he filled out the application. In fact, everyone had been supportive, except one person: Cat.

She was standing in front of him, her arms crossed beneath her breasts. She had dressed as she normally did: t-shirt and cargo pants. She had her sidearm in the hip holster, and her hair up in a ponytail. She had no idea just how damned sexy and powerful she looked. For a minute, the moment after Del and Emma's wedding came rushing back to him. He stole Cat away from the dance floor so they could be alone. The scents and the sounds were still so tangible; it was as if it happened yesterday. It had been just a hallway off the lanai where the wedding was being held. In that one blinding instant, he had been sure it was the beginning of something wonderful.

She was laughing when he'd kissed her.

"Hey, Drew, wake up."

The woman who had stolen his heart was now staring at him and snapping her fingers in his face.

He scowled at her. "I'm awake."

She studied him before saying, "Now, when you get to the office, make sure you don't give yourself away."

"I know."

"If you have a hinky feeling, you need to get out of there. Just leave."

She was talking to him like he was an idiot. He had a slow boiling temper, but when it got going, it was dangerous to everyone around him.

Cat apparently picked up on it. "Don't give me that look, Drew. Pay attention."

"I know what to do, Cat."

"I just want to make sure you understand that we don't want to blow your cover completely because, you know, legal issues."

That was too much. He might not be on the investigation side of the house, where he would go out into the field, but he was not a damned imbecile. "Jesus, woman, I'm going in for an appointment. It's not like I'll get killed at the offices of Premiere Connections."

"I know that. But remember, don't deny you work here."

It was as if he hadn't said anything. "I filled out the application and put down that I work here. Makes it kind of hard to deny after the fact."

She sighed. "Sorry. I know I shouldn't be such a pain in the ass, but I can't help it. I want to make sure you stay safe."

Her concern had his emotions all twisted. Why was she doing this now? Was it just the job or something else? And why the hell did he care? He had given up caring, right?

He pushed aside all of that and turned away.

"Drew?"

"Seeing that all the men were killed in their own homes, that won't be a problem for me. I'm not going to be taking them home with me. But, dinner out might give us some insight. Just like Del said."

When she didn't say anything, he glanced over his shoulder at her. She still didn't look convinced.

"I can handle a date, Cat. Or even two or three. Don't worry."

"I'm just not comfortable with you going on these dates. We don't have the names of the women yet."

"Didn't you get the warrant?"

She rolled her eyes. "We went to the wrong judge first. He's apparently signed up for the service, but did not recuse himself. We had to file again, and we should get the warrant any time now."

"So, then we can compare it to my dates and see if it works out."

"Yeah, we might just find out that you don't match up with their women."

"The one thing that bothers me—and this is not from experience, but from what I read about these kinds of computer programs— but they should pick up on similarities."

Her eyes narrowed as she studied him. Having that much attention from Cat usually caused him to lose most of the blood in his brain.

"What do you mean?"

"I'm sure Charity can explain it better."

"No. Tell me. If I still don't understand, I'll go to Charity for the computer dating for dummies version."

Dammit, he hated when she talked herself down like that. He knew that her mother did not value Cat's intelligence as much as she should.

"You are not stupid. It's that I don't express myself well sometimes."

She snorted.

He let it go, although it still bothered him.

"Anyway, from what I have been reading on this, you fill out your basic application. They all have similar algorithms that help each person find matches."

"Where are you going with this?"

"All four of these men were so different. They had different interests. Their ages alone would make you think they'd have different dates. I would think that if they dated the same women, we wouldn't have too many to go through."

"I get it. You think because they wouldn't have that many similarities, they would only have a couple women who would match up to all of them. Good point."

"Maybe we will only have to find a couple of women to

check out. That might make it really easy."

"When has anything with us ever been easy?" she joked.

"Almost never." His voice had deepened as he continued to stare at her. Her smile faded and, just like that, the air between them thickened. He couldn't look away, and didn't want to. Of course, like always, she broke the contact. He drew in a deep breath.

"I'm on my way," he said, slipping the earpiece into his ear. "See ya later, Cat."

He left without another word, or even waiting for her to say anything else to him. It was only the first day of this, and he was already overwhelmed. He was almost out the door, when he saw Autumn, their new team member. She smiled at him.

"Hey, I haven't gotten to talk to you. My name's Autumn." Then she rolled her eyes. "Of course, you know that. You were at the meeting yesterday, and I sound like a server at TGI Fridays. Anyway, I take it you're Drew, right?"

"Yeah," he said smiling. It was hard not to. "Are you getting settled in?"

"Sort of. I'm glad I'm not jumping on a case."

"That is never fun, although, this is the first one I've worked on like this."

"Oh, right, you're going to sign up for the dating service."

He nodded. "About to head out right now."

"I'll let you go then. I just thought I would introduce myself. Good luck."

"Thanks, I'm going to need it."

He was turning to leave when he caught a glimpse of Cat out of the corner of his eye. The frown she was sending his way told him all he needed to know. He was going to be late if he didn't get out of there, and they couldn't have that.

He hurried out the door, his mind on the meeting. The

sooner he got this over with, the sooner he could be rid of Cat and all the distractions she caused.

# CHAPTER SEVEN

Drew was right on time for his appointment at Premiere Connections. He found the office to be a bit stifling, and the questionnaires stupid. Even after filling out the application, and making his own dorky video on his computer, he still had more crap to fill out. All the questions were worse than the application. How was someone supposed to find a soulmate when the questions seemed to center around money? It wasn't overt, but most of them were focused around how much he was worth. It had left him feeling vaguely irritated, not to mention sad for the people who used the services.

"Mr. Franklin?"

Drew looked up and found the receptionist smiling at him. She stood by the side of her desk, a clipboard in her hands, as she waited for him to respond.

"Yes?"

"Ms. Collins is ready for you."

He blinked. "Ms. Collins? The owner?"

A few of the other men looked up from their questionnaires. From their expressions, this was probably odd. Why would the owner of the company want to meet with him? Did she know that he was sent in to check them out? Dammit. Irritation and panic twisted his gut. He wanted to help the investigation, so he tried his best not to let any emotion show on his face. Plus, there was the side benefit of proving Cat wrong.

She nodded, her brown curls bouncing with the movement. "Yes. Come on."

He rose from his chair and followed her through the door to a long hallway.

"Ms. Collins is very interested in meeting you."

"Is that a fact?"

She tossed a killer smile over her shoulder. "All of us love your family restaurants."

Of course. "Which one is your favorite?" he asked. It was expected. If he didn't ask, people usually told him.

"I love the North Shore Grill. They have the best fish tacos."

"I have to agree with that."

As she continued to rattle on about her favorite dishes from the family restaurants, he followed her silently. All the women who worked at Premiere—and it appeared only women worked there—wore brightly colored Hawaiian print dresses. The receptionist was wearing a dark pink version. It would look normal except it came off feeling inauthentic to him. He couldn't figure out why, but everything seemed fake.

Maybe it was the surroundings. They had what would be considered catnip for someone who loved it that way, but it seemed weird. The photographs that depicted gorgeous views of Hawaii looked out of place on stark white walls. It was…odd. Everything was stark in the décor, except for those pictures hung on the walls.

She opened the door and let him into a room. Hawaiian decor, but it seemed off somehow. It was as if whoever decorated it went shopping for what they *thought* Hawaiians would like. Blue walls, a plush couch, and all the little things most mainlanders identified as authentic Hawaiian décor.

"Here you go, Mr. Franklin. Ms. Collins will be here any minute."

She left him in the room, and he took a moment to look around. Drew knew better than to do anything that would raise anyone's suspicions. There was a pretty good chance there were recording devices in the room.

"This place is weird," he said. Cat and Graeme could hear him, but he couldn't hear their comments. "Not too sure what this proves, but I don't get a real pleasant vibe."

He walked around looking at the pictures of happy couples. None had names, so there was always a chance they could be stock photos. In fact, one was a young Asian couple smiling into the camera. He was sure he had seen it before in an ad online.

A pitcher of cucumber water sat on a table, so he decided to help himself. He had just taken a sip, when the door opened.

"Mr. Franklin, I'm so happy to meet you."

Her turned at the sound of the female voice, and felt his eyes widen. She was the average height for a model, but that was the only thing that was average about her. Long curly blonde hair framed a heart-shaped face. She wasn't wearing one of the Hawaiian dresses like the rest of the women who worked there. She wore a simple pink dress that hugged her curves. The perfect cupid's bow mouth was glossed, which wasn't the most appealing thing about her.

Blue would be the color of her eyes, but that didn't do them justice. There was something otherworldly about the shade. A hint of amethyst rimmed the outer edges.

"Mr. Franklin?"

He shook his head, trying to bring himself back to reality. He cleared his throat.

"Thank you, Ms. Collins."

"Please, call me Alice."

"Only if you call me Drew."

She smiled, showing two perfect dimples. He couldn't

do anything but respond in kind. Damn, for a second, his brain stopped working. He knew it was probably something she was accustomed to. Women like her knew their effect on people, and there was no doubt Alice knew. Beyond just being beautiful, she had a waiting room full of clients. Smart and beautiful. It wasn't easy to ignore a woman who was looking at you as if you were her favorite treat. Of course, he reminded himself, he was. The woman was looking for rich men to use to make herself rich.

"I'm a big fan of your family restaurants. I love the Hawaiian Lunch Kitchen over in Kailua."

Right. Everyone always mentioned the restaurants. "I worked at that one all through high school. I like it a lot better now that I'm not behind the counter."

She chuckled. "I can imagine. I'm not very good at cooking, so I would be useless in the kitchen. I did wait tables in college, though. I didn't like it very much."

"Yeah, not the most fun job. Of course, being good in the kitchen isn't the most important thing I look for in a woman."

Her smile widened even more, which sent a few alarm bells off in his head.

"I see that I am not going to have a problem getting you any dates. Smart, sexy, and very accommodating."

He felt his face heat when he remembered that they were recording the conversation at TFH. He was just thankful they couldn't make extra recordings of it. That would be ten times worse than Cat and Graeme telling the team. But there was one thing that was for sure: they *would* tell the others.

"So, why don't we get started, okay?" she said as she sat down beside him.

He nodded, wishing this day was over. The guys weren't going to ever let him live this down.

Cat shifted as she listened through the headphones and bit back a growl. This Alice woman was laying it on thick. All this gushing over Drew was calculated. She'd barely wanted to talk to Graeme. It almost made her sick just having to listen to it. She ground her teeth together.

"She's a lot nicer to him than she was to us," Graeme said. She glanced at him.

Yeah, she was. In fact, if Cat didn't know this was about getting him a date, she would say this Collins woman was trying to pick Drew up. Or get him to pay for the night. The woman was an operator, there was no doubt about it. What kind of operator, Cat wasn't sure. It could be that she was just trying to sell the company and not herself. Drew would clearly be a feather in PC's cap. His family had a lot of clout on the island.

"He *is* a paying customer."

Graeme shrugged. "Just saying."

For some reason, hearing Graeme say the phrase in his thick Scottish accent, made her smile.

"Now, Drew, I understand you are looking to use our service. You know about all the fees?" Alice asked.

"Yes," Drew said. "I already signed and paid the initial payment."

"You need to make sure that Del pays him back," Graeme said.

She nodded, but was barely paying any attention.

"Cat?"

"What?" she asked, irritated because she couldn't hear what was going on. Truthfully, they only needed to listen for anything suspicious. She just didn't like the way the woman was acting. Collins seemed intent on getting his attention and making him feel as if she were his personal servant.

"You need to make sure that he gets paid back."

"I can try, but there is a good chance he won't take the money," she said.

"Bollocks."

"No. He really has a lot of money, and won't let people pay him back. *Ever.*"

"Rich?"

"Yeah. *Really* rich. The family has a lot of land and a lot of restaurants. I think they even plan on opening some on the mainland this year. I believe in Vegas."

"So, in your ideal mate, can you give me an idea about what you would like?"

"I filled out the application."

"Yes, I saw. I wondered if there was anything for you to add."

He said nothing and, knowing him like she did, Cat was sure that he just shook his head.

"Okay. We'll activate your account, and you can start looking through the prospects. I hope that you are happy with everything."

"That's it?"

"Yes."

"Then why did I have to come in here?"

There was a beat of silence, and Cat couldn't fight the smile. It wasn't like Drew to be so rude, but he was playing a part. A wealthy man might be a bit of a dick and complain about something like that. Drew never would, but then, his mother raised him properly.

"I like to meet with our most preferred clients to get to know them."

"Oh, okay. Well, I will let you know if I need anything."

*"Please do," Alice responded.* Then they heard him stand and walk out of the room.

"That was a little odd, right?" Cat said as she set her headphones aside.

"A bit, but…does he really have a lot of money?"

Cat shrugged. "I guess so. I always assumed because his family is an institution on the island. I don't know anyone who grew up here who didn't eat at one of their restaurants. He also went to Punahou."

"I always forget about that, probably because he doesn't act like he has money. Oh, hey, there he is."

She turned and caught a glimpse of Drew as he passed by in his car. They had purposely made sure not to show even the hint that they knew he was in there for a meeting. They wanted it to look like what they said. Her phone pinged and she looked down to read Adam's text.

Got the search warrant. *-Adam*

Thank God.

Good. We are about to head back. Got someone you can take with you to serve it?

Yeah, Marcus is here.

Good, report if there are any problems.

"I guess we should go back to the office and start going through the lists. Hopefully, one of these chicks will be on there."

Graeme chuckled.

"What?"

"You always call women chicks."

Not her friends, or women she respected, but these women…okay it wasn't fair. She didn't know these women at all, but that didn't make it any easier to ignore what was happening. Pushing aside those thoughts, she started up the SUV and headed back to the office.

"They should be able to get the names with the search warrant," Graeme said.

"Yeah. We will just have the names of the women that the victims dated. That's it."

"And then Drew can set up the dates?" Graeme asked.

Cat tightened her hands on the steering wheel. Of course, Graeme wanted to talk about the case. She wanted to wallow in self-pity for just a second or two.

"Yeah. We'll compare those names with our list and match any dates Drew gets paired up with."

"He may not get matched up with someone from our list."

"True."

But she knew her luck…or lack thereof. She had no doubt they would have at least one or two matches. As she turned onto Ala Moana Boulevard, Cat started thinking about the interview. She would never admit it out loud, but she knew part of her irritation with this entire thing was because she was jealous. She knew what it was like to have Drew's attention, and she had thrown it away. Like an idiot. Like she always did. She was her own worst enemy.

All she had to do was not make a fool of herself, and maybe, she would survive this mess.

Drew had just finished using the free weights when he walked over to where TJ was doing squats.

"So, Charity said you have to go undercover."

Since they were the only ones in the condo's gym, Drew figured it was okay.

"Yeah, it's weird."

"Yeah. Undercover always sucks."

"Especially at a dating service."

"Yeah? What is that place like?"

"Did Charity tell you about it?"

"A little bit, but she hasn't been inside. I've heard about it for the last few months."

That was news to him. "In what context?"

"HPD wanted our help at looking at them for running a call-in service for call girls."

"I can see that."

"Yeah?"

He nodded as he went over to the shoulder machine. He sat down on the bench and wrapped his fingers around the bar and started his repetitions.

"Only women work there. And they all dress alike."

"That was one of the reasons, and the amount of

money they make. It drew a lot of red flags. But even with both our forensic accountant and theirs digging through the books, they couldn't find anything suspicious."

Drew finished his tenth repetition, he looked over at TJ. "Nothing at all?"

"Yeah, why?"

"It is statistically impossible to find absolutely nothing suspect when someone is keeping the books for a business. Humans make errors."

TJ shrugged. "Not sure what to tell you, man. They just said they found nothing."

"Either way, that place is creepy. Like Stepford wives' kind of creepy."

TJ chuckled. "How is it working with Cat?"

"I guess okay. I suppose Charity told you that Cat didn't want me on the case?"

"Yeah, but that has to do with her feelings, and I'm sure it was just a knee jerk reaction to you being on the case."

"And she thinks I can't handle it."

"No, I think it's because she doesn't want you hurt."

"Charity said the same thing."

"I don't know what to tell you, because you know how much I almost fucked up with Charity. But I would side with the women in your office. They're smarter than any man I know."

"Did Charity tell you to say that?"

He chuckled. "No, but it does sound like something she would say."

"And she would be right."

"Just keep an open mind."

"I closed that door six months ago."

"Up to you, but if she's still bothering you, then there is a good chance something was there."

Something would always be there. He might have moved on, but he would always feel something for the woman who let him kiss her breathless on the dance floor.

MELISSA SCHROEDER

# CHAPTER EIGHT

Drew had just gotten out of the shower and barely had his clothes on when his doorbell rang. It was odd that anyone would show up unannounced, since they had a security system in the building. He walked to the door and looked out the peephole. When he saw Cat standing in the hallway, it was a swift kick to the gut.

What the hell was she doing here? He wanted to pretend he wasn't home, but that was the coward's way out. Plus, she had excellent hearing. There was a good chance she heard him approach the door. He drew in a breath and released it slowly before opening the door.

"Hey, what are you doing here?"

She blinked, probably because he had been a little harsh in his tone.

"I have the list and I thought you would want it," she said. "I thought it would be easier to go through the list here than at the office."

"You could have called."

"I did. You didn't answer."

He frowned and turned around to grab his phone. Five missed calls. All within fifteen minutes. He looked up at her.

"Sorry. I was working out and then I was in the shower."

She said nothing. She kept looking up at him with her

golden-brown gaze. A few seconds ticked by, mainly because whenever he made eye contact, his thoughts scattered. It didn't matter that it had been over a year since they'd kissed, or that she had made it clear she saw him only as a friend. All he wanted to do was lean closer and touch his mouth to hers.

"Drew?"

It was then that he realized he wasn't only blocking the doorway, but he was also leaning towards her.

"You need to move so I can get in."

He hesitated, then said, "Come on in. We can go over the names and pick out the ones on the list."

"If you would rather I not be here, I can just give you the list," she said, holding up the paper. Hurt flashed in her eyes before it disappeared. And for a long split second, he wanted to grab the paper and tell her to leave. It would keep him from hurting every time he looked at her. That wouldn't solve anything. If they were going to survive, they had to learn to work together. He knew they both loved their jobs and wouldn't want to work anywhere else. It was imperative they learn how to deal with each other.

"I said come in."

He waited, then she finally stepped over the threshold. He closed the door and followed her into the living room. It was the polite thing to do, but it was almost worse than making eye contact with her. It was hard to ignore that sassy stride of hers. It wasn't the kind of walk where she thought men were looking. It was a defiant...I can kick your ass if I want...saunter. Most men wouldn't find it sexy, but Drew did. Dammit.

"Wow, this really looks a lot better," she said, looking around the living room.

It was then he realized she hadn't been up there since Emma had fought off a serial killer. It had been her apartment, and Drew had moved in a few months earlier, after Emma was already living with Del. It had had some damage, but Emma had wanted it completely redone. It had prime views, overlooking the ocean, and being within a quick walk to work.

"Yeah, I think Emma's brother Sean took care of it all."

She smiled. "Okay, let's get down to business, then I can get out of your way."

"No rush. I need some water. Want anything to drink?"

She shook her head as she sat on the sofa. He had his computer sitting on the coffee table. As he grabbed a glass of water, he heard the telltale sign of Cat's mother's text ringer.

Cat made a sound of irritation.

"Problems with your mother?" he asked as he sat down beside her. She tensed, then relaxed.

She shrugged. "Nothing new."

"Did she really call Del?"

Cat closed her eyes, then opened them. "Yes. She thought I might be dead."

Drew chuckled. Cat's mother was a bit overbearing, but she did care about her daughter. In a dictator kind of way.

"Nothing wrong?"

She sighed. "My sister. Marie. She wants to get married. Mom thinks she is too young."

Drew frowned. "You aren't that much older, and she is always after you to get married."

"Thanks for the reminder," she said.

"Sorry. But you know it's true."

It was one of the things that had irritated him the most about Cat's family. They never understood her need to work in law enforcement. Like everyone else on TFH, she had her reasons for being on the team, but when you boiled it down, they all believed in justice. It was so ingrained in her character, that he couldn't see Cat doing anything else. Until now, he had always been on the outside of the investigation. He would assist Elle, and sit in on meetings. Now, though, he was starting to understand just how much she did.

"And why is it wrong that Marie is thinking of getting married?"

She jerked her shoulder. "I dunno. You know my mother. She wants control. I don't want to get married so she makes my life a living hell. My sister wants to get married, same result. I'm just happy she's not bugging me."

"You don't need a man to make you complete. You're an amazing detective, and she should be proud of your career."

She stopped what she was doing and turned her head. "Thank you," she said.

He nodded. "Nothing but the truth."

She swallowed, then cleared her throat. "So, these are the women. I'm hoping that at least one or two of them are on your list.

He nodded and pulled up his account. He had a picture of him on the beach, his surfboard next to him, and he was, of course, only wearing a pair of board shorts. Cat said nothing for a long moment, then she glanced at him.

"Who took the pic?"

"Charity."

"Ah. Well, it's good."

"I feel like a dork for posting it, but she said it was good."

"It is. You seem to have put on a little weight."

There was a suspicious quiver in her voice, and he glanced at her. She was still staring at the account as if nothing was going on, so he mentally shrugged it off.

He leaned closer to the screen, and he could smell her then. That unique scent of herbal soap and Cat. He cleared his throat.

"Let's see. Okay, there are three…no, four matches here. No, wait. Five. That's odd."

"Why?" she asked.

"I still find it weird that the four men, and now me have so many women in common."

"Do you think it's on purpose?"

"Charity would be best to know about that. She might be able to get into their system and see if it is a set up."

"Why would someone do that?"

He shrugged. "Not sure."

"I don't think that has anything to do with the murders."

"But?"

She glanced at him, her golden brown eyes a little unfocused, as he knew she was thinking about the job. Jesus, how was he finding every damned thing she was doing sexy? But it was. Watching her work something out in her head always made him a little crazy.

"Do you think it might have more to do with potential earnings?"

He blinked. "What?"

"Maybe these women were looking for men who are in a higher tax bracket."

"But isn't everyone who goes there rich?"

"No. There are some men who sign up who are upper middle class. They don't turn them away, but they might only allow men like you to get hooked up with one of these women."

He thought about that, and looked back at the screen. "So, probably not anything to do with the murders. I wonder if the women pay extra."

"Good point. It might be that, or it might be that Ms. Collins knows these women. It's definitely something to keep in mind."

"Okay, so do we have any guide?"

"What do you mean?" she asked.

"Like, do we know who he dated last?"

"No. Charity said Branson hadn't officially gone out with any of these women in a week. Although, she is still going through the data. The others were further back; Waters was over a year ago. As a result, it is going to require some digging. Right now, there isn't much in the file other than he had been a client. Premiere Connections said closed accounts are deleted."

"Are you all going to question the women?"

"Yes. In particular, these five. But I think Del is right. We need to do a little investigating, and you dating them is the quickest way. If we go asking friends and family, they'll find out about it."

Just hearing that he had to go on dates made him itch. He didn't mind helping on the case. "But just because they all went out with these same women, doesn't mean anything."

"The only thing these four men had in common were these five women. There was one other who dated the first three victims, but she is living on the mainland now and married."

"All of us were matched up with these women?"

"Yes."

"You know what else is odd?"

"What?"

"I don't know any of them, do you?"

She looked over at the screen and shook her head. "That *is* odd. I mean, I know there are 850,000 people on this island, but between the two of us, we should know at least one of them.

He nodded. He pulled up the first name. Lana Cho. He started to message her, but Cat stopped him.

"Why this one?"

"She's in alphabetical order," he said.

She made a little choking sound, but said nothing. He looked over and found her smiling.

"Sorry, forgot."

"What did you forget?" he asked.

Her smile faded. "Nothing, don't worry."

"No. Tell me."

"You have to do everything in order."

"So?"

She shook her head. "I always thought it was cute.

Never mind. Go ahead and finish your message."

He didn't know what to say, so he did just that. He wrote a short message and sent it off.

"Should I do all of them now, or should I wait—"

The ping signaling that he had a message sounded.

"Well, that was fast," Cat murmured.

He leaned closer, then hesitated.

"What are you waiting on?"

"Sorry, just odd that I have someone looking over my shoulder like this."

He opened the message. Lana agreed to meet.

"How about tomorrow night?" Drew asked.

"No. Make it Saturday."

"Why wait another day?"

"First, it will make her think you have other plans, and not just sitting around. Second, you give her the impression that you don't think she is sitting around waiting for a date. And third, it gives us time to do background checks on her and talk to friends and family of the victims. We are still trying to round up interviews from some of them."

"Okay." He wrote up a short note, offered to take her to dinner on Saturday. She immediately responded with a yes.

"There you go. It's all set up," he said. She said nothing, so he turned his head and looked at her. She did not look too happy.

"Is something wrong?"

She shook her head. "No. Nothing. Listen, I gotta go. We'll do background checks on all the other women so you can contact them next week."

"Okay. Sure."

She stood and headed toward the door.

"Did I do something wrong?"

She shook her head, her pony tail swaying with the motion. "No. All good. I'll see you tomorrow."

Before he could say anything else, she was out the door

and hurrying down the hall. Frowning, he closed the door and stood there for a long time.

There was no way he was ever going to understand women.

Cat was almost to her car when her mother texted again. She wanted to ignore it, but her mother wasn't going to allow for that. Plus, Del might not be so understanding this time around if she called him.

She dialed her mother's number and, of course, she picked up on the first ring. "Finally. Have you talked to Marie?"

She should have known that was what her mother was calling about. "No. I've been just a little busy."

"Busy doing what? Are you not at home?"

"No. I just got done with work. I'm about to go home."

"So, you can call her now."

She sighed. "No. I will try to do it tomorrow."

"Why not tonight?"

She sighed, even knowing it would irritate her mother. When her mother was in this state of mind, everything irritated her. "Because I'm busy."

"What could you do that is more important than helping your family?"

"Well, I don't know. Maybe it's the fact that I haven't eaten since lunch. Or maybe it's that I'm chasing a serial killer on my first ever lead on a case. But you didn't ask about that, Mom."

There was a beat of silence from her mother, and from a few people in the parking garage who were now staring at her. Great. That was professional.

"Listen, I promise I will talk to her as soon as I can. But, you know, Marie. She's got a mind of her own. The more you push, the more she will cling to that loser more."

"So you agree. He's a loser."

She couldn't help but chuckle. "I've met him once, so I will reserve judgement. But I will talk to her."

"You have a lead on the case?"

"Yeah, I do."

"That's…good."

That was high praise coming from her mother. "I have to start driving and I don't like being on the phone."

"Okay, Catherine, I will talk to you tomorrow."

Not if she could avoid it.

"And, call your sister tomorrow."

"Bye, Mom."

She clicked her phone off and got into the SUV. As she started up the vehicle, she pushed thoughts of her mother and sister aside. Of course, that just caused her to think about her time with Drew tonight. This wasn't going to be easy. It was bad enough she wanted to smack that stupid Autumn for smiling at him, but now she had to listen in on his dates.

She closed her eyes. God, this was going to be horrible. He had smiled at her tonight—like he had before he'd been shot—and she'd wanted to do nothing more than kiss him. To feel that powerful rush like she'd had before…to lose herself in pleasure.

She could still remember the way it felt when he kissed her. Her knees had gone weak, and she'd felt slightly off balanced every time he did it. It had been the most amazing feeling in the world. And tonight, when he had leaned closer, she had been pushed back into those heady memories of their one night.

Opening her eyes, she brought herself back from that insanity. She wasn't made for relationships. She had proven that by walking out on him when he was hurt, then ignoring him during his recovery. He was a man who deserved someone who could be there for him, and she had proven to herself and everyone else she didn't have it in her.

With that thought, she backed out of the parking space and headed home. She had some background checks to perform, and she still had a killer to catch.

# CHAPTER NINE

The next morning came too early for Cat. She had spent another night working and woke up with her face on her laptop keyboard. She was sure if someone looked close enough, they would be able to see the impressions of the keys on her cheek. Add in the insanely hot dreams she'd had all featuring Drew, and she was just a little bit more than cranky.

Now she had to talk to the Andersons. The idea of talking to a grieving family left her irritated and just a little guilty. Which made her even crankier. It was self-centered to think about herself and her feelings while these people had lost someone they loved.

She scrubbed her hand over her face, trying to force herself to wake up. Anderson's sons would arrive any minute. Walking over to the coffeemaker, she smiled at a scowling Graeme. She poured herself a cup of Kona, and made her way over to Graeme's doorway.

"What's wrong?"

"I married a shrew."

She chuckled. "No, you didn't."

"I want her to use some of her maternity leave before the baby comes."

"Please tell me you didn't call her old again."

"I never called her old. I said that for the safety of our child, she might just want to rest before the birth."

"Oh, Graeme," she said chuckling. "If I didn't know you loved her so much, I'd want to slap you. Take my advice and just lay off it for a while."

"I'm just worried about the *bairn*."

"*Bairn* means baby, right?"

He nodded and she smiled.

"I know you are, and Elle knows, too. But, do you think she would do anything that would jeopardize the baby? I know she lost a baby before, but she has made it to the third trimester this time. She's going to be fine. If you just give her a little space, she might calm down and stop calling you a goat."

He sighed. "Thanks."

She saw two men walk in, side-by-side. There was no mistaking they were Branson Anderson's sons. Tall, tanned, with his thick wavy hair and steel blue eyes, the men didn't fall far from the tree. Both had the good looks and amazing stature of athletes.

"I'll see you later," she said as she watched Anderson's sons walk toward her.

She stepped out of the office.

"Hello," she said.

"We're John and Harry Anderson. We're looking for Detective Kalakau."

"That would be me. We can talk in my office."

They followed her, then she stepped aside so they could both enter ahead of her. Once they were seated, she asked, "Would you like something to drink?"

They both shook their heads. She looked at the one that spoke. He had black hair and was just slightly taller than the other son. "I guess you're John and," she said looking at the other man, "you're Harry."

They nodded.

"I'm sure you have talked to Commander Delano about all the particulars, but we wanted to talk with you further."

"I'm not sure what we can give you. We've both been on the mainland for work," Harry said.

"You worked with your father, right?"

They both nodded.

"We handled most of the PR for the company, so we were on the mainland talking to some athletes about sponsorship."

She nodded. "How long were you off the island?"

"The last three weeks," John said. "We can give you dates and locations."

"That would help. We need to eliminate everyone. Can you tell me if there was anything strange lately about your father?"

"No," John said. "In fact, he was just getting out and dating again."

"Yeah," Harry said. "We were both really happy about it. Mom's death hit him hard, and he hadn't really showed any interest. We'd joke that he was going to turn into the weird old dude who lives on the hill."

"About that, did he tell you anything about those dates? Anything weird or off about any of the women?"

They looked at each other, then looked back at Cat.

"What do you mean?" John asked.

"Just anything off about any of the women he dated. Did any of them seem a little too interested in your father?"

"You think a woman did this? One of the ones he went out with?" the younger brother asked.

She shook he head. "I can't say anything more than that. We're still looking at everyone in his life, but usually, when there is a murder, there is some incident that causes a ripple effect. Something that puts them in contact with the killer."

"I can't think of anything," John said.

"The flowers," his brother murmured.

"What?" Cat said.

"He got flowers the other day," Harry said. "I was talking to him on the phone and they arrived at the house."

"Did he say who they were from or what kind?"

"Roses. They were red roses," Harry said. "He laughed it off, but even over the phone, it made me think that he was uneasy with the idea. I thought it was just because it's odd for a guy to get flowers, you know?"

"Do you think that might be a clue?" John asked.

"I can't say until we check it out. Do you know when they were delivered?"

"He had several deliveries over the last few weeks, but I know the last one arrived two days before he was...before he died. He might have thrown them out, but they would still be in the trash. We can check it out," Harry offered.

Cat shook her head. "No, don't worry about that. We have the trash and will look for flowers. Do you have any other questions or any information that you think might help?"

"I can't think of anything," John said. "This is just so surreal. When Mom died, we were ready for it. Or at least prepared, this...Dad was in such good shape, so you don't get expect something like this to happen."

She had grown up without her father, so she knew that could be tough. But in such a short span of time to lose both parents, it was unimaginable.

"Thank you both for coming in. I promise that I will keep you up to date as much as possible."

The men nodded as they stood. As he was walking out, John stopped. "Just promise me you will find that bastard who did this."

"I am going to do everything in my power to find justice for your father."

He nodded, then headed out the door behind his brother.

She sat behind her desk and started to think over the

case. The notes and flowers were a link between this case and the last. Since Anderson had just died, there was a good chance that there might be a trail for them to follow. She pulled up the report and located the note about garbage. There was nothing there, but it didn't mean that whoever sent them didn't take them after the murder. The fact that it wasn't listed with the other crime scene reports certainly made it a possibility.

Cat grabbed her phone and clicked on Charity's number. It was better to be safe than sorry.

"Good afternoon, Ms. Cat. Did you need something?"

"I was looking over the crime scene report. There were no flowers or notes, right?"

"Right, and I double checked the list again after Adam and Marcus found that link. Was there a reason you are asking now?"

"Anderson's sons said they had the same issue."

"And that makes it a link. I checked all the crime scene reports from the other murders. No flowers."

"Thanks."

"I hear that Drew has a date tomorrow night."

She ground her teeth together, and tried not to growl. "Yeah. And thanks for helping him set up his account."

"That boy doesn't know how to make the most of what he has. I filled out just about everything. Or, I should say, I told him what to put down. And I forced him to use that picture. He didn't think it was a good idea."

"Yeah, again, thanks for that and for the info."

"You got it."

After she clicked off the phone, she pulled up the smart screen and looked at the info they had on each man. Unfortunately, her focus was now shot. Dammit.

All she could think about was that stupid date Drew had scheduled for tomorrow night. She decided she needed another cup of coffee to get her head screwed on straight, but she wanted a treat. She needed a sugar rush.

As she was walking to the door, she caught a glimpse

of Del in his office with Tamilya Lowe. The former FBI agent was well versed in terrorism, especially of the homegrown types. From their body language, it looked like an interview.

"Yeah, I saw her show up when you were talking to the Anderson brothers," Graeme said.

"I take it she wants to work on TFH?"

"Yeah. Or, more likely, Del went after her. The woman has contacts within the security industry, both civilian and government, that are a goldmine for information."

"This could make life really interesting around here," she said.

"How did the interview go?"

"Good, got a little bit more information. I was going to go out and get a frozen coffee, then come back and work it out."

"Mind if I join you? I was scheduled for testimony today for the Henderson case, but they made a deal. We can chat it over."

She smiled. "That would be great. I just needed to get out of the office."

"Great, and I'll even buy."

"You win the day," she said with a laugh, as she followed him out the door and into the stuffy hallway and then outside into the warm sunlight.

"Did they give you any more insight to what was going on with their father?" Graeme asked as the walked side by side.

"Not really, but he did get flowers and notes. They didn't see them, and their father tried to laugh it off. They both think he was a little freaked out by it."

"So, that is one connection with all of them."

She nodded. "I need you to run a check on flower deliveries. We'll need to start small and expand."

"Let's start with anyone who delivers to Kailua. Since he's the last one, it would be easier to get receipts."

She nodded. "Roses. They all probably got the same

thing, but one of the sons said it was roses. Those are a pretty penny so make sure to use that as a reference."

Graeme nodded as they approached the line for the coffee cart. As they stood there, she saw the Anderson brothers drive down the street that led to Ala Moana Boulevard. Having lost a parent herself, she knew what was probably going through their minds. The pain of losing their only parent would be first. The grief would be overwhelming. But soon, anger would take over.

She vowed that they would have answers for them. No one should have to go through this and at least not know who murdered their father.

Drew was heading out the door when he noticed that Cat's light was still on in her office. He should leave, but something lured him over to her. There was no reason he should stop in, but he couldn't seem to keep himself from going. Mainly because he was an idiot.

She was sitting at her desk, her back to the door as she looked things over on her computer. She must have noticed him in the reflection of her computer screen.

"Hey," she said, turning around. "Did you need something?"

He shook his head. "Just noticed your light. I stayed late and finished up some reports for Elle."

"Yeah, she didn't look good today."

"She hasn't been sleeping well."

Cat nodded. "Talked to Branson Anderson's sons today. They both said nothing was odd, but someone was sending him flowers."

"Flowers?"

"Yeah, like bouquets. Like on the other report we had. But I went through the inventory, and there is nothing in the house or trash about flowers. According to one of the sons, he got them right before he was murdered. Trash hadn't been picked up. They should be somewhere, but they aren't."

"Odd."

"Yeah, so that is definitely something to consider further. We have yet to hear back from the others with any information. I've got a call in to Rome about it." Rome Carino was a detective for the HPD and their liaison.

He glanced at her computer and saw his date for Saturday night. He felt an itch between his shoulder blades. It shouldn't bother him that Cat knew he had a date, or that she would be listening in on it. It was just a bit creepy. And it made him feel guilty. He had no idea why, but it did.

"Yeah, I was checking out your girl."

"She's not my girl." He studied Cat trying to discern her mood, but he couldn't. "And?"

She shrugged. "Seems normal enough. Thirty, works as a phlebotomist for some clinic over in Aiea."

"Is she from Oahu?"

"No. She's from Maui. And that is another thing. The other four women all came from other islands or the mainland."

"Odd. That's why we didn't recognize any of them."

"Yeah. Very odd. But Cho has a long history in Maui, well known. Family has deep roots. She dated all four victims, but she went out with Branson three times, from what we can tell."

"Hmm, wasn't he a little old for her?"

Cat chuckled. "No. All of his dates were in their late twenties or early thirties. Not *that* many years' difference, although, I think one of them was the same age as his sons."

"I don't understand that."

"You haven't had a midlife crisis. Maybe you will."

He shook his head. "Well, if there's nothing else?"

"Not really. The warrant came through for the

surveillance. I doubt anything will result in an arrest, but it could give us leads, so we covered our asses. Do you want to be here or at your place to get wired up for your date tomorrow night?"

There was no way he wanted to get ready at his condo. It would be too intimate. It was bad enough that she had been there the other night. "Here. I think it will be easier. Plus, just in case anyone is watching, they will think I just stopped by work on my way to the date."

"Very smart. It was going to be my suggestion too, but I wanted it to be wherever you were comfortable."

He nodded. "See you tomorrow night, then."

"Around five work?"

"Yep. Good night," he said, forcing himself to leave. The need to stay there just to be close to her was a bit pathetic. He needed to be with her on some level that he just didn't understand. He should be happy that they seemed to have found a way to work together, that it didn't hurt him just to look at her. Drew knew he had to continue to keep his distance, even if every instinct told him to go back to her.

With a shake of his head, he headed out the door, glad he had walked to work that morning. He lived close enough he could walk, and he needed the fresh air to clear his senses.

This was one of his favorite times of day. The sun dipped over the horizon with just the hint of orange glow dancing off the waves, and the sweet scent of plumeria hung in the air. As he crossed the street, Charity's ringtone rang from his phone.

He turned down Ala Moana and headed to his condo before he pulled it out and answered.

"Hey, Charity."

"Hey yourself. Aren't you home yet?"

"Nope. I stayed after to finish a little bit of work."

"So, what are you wearing tomorrow?"

"I'm not a girl who is going to obsess over what to

wear on a date."

She snorted. "Are you being derogatory to women?"

"No. Just different creatures."

But now that she commented on it, he started to wonder what to wear. Absolutely not the shirt he had on today. It read: Screw your lab safety. I want my superpowers. For some reason, he thought that might not impress a woman who was accustomed to dates with Premiere Connections.

"And, you just called us creatures."

He heard someone murmur in the background, and knew it was TJ, Charity's fiancé, and known to some as Hammer.

"I don't care what you think. He's being rude." Another murmur from TJ. "No. I am not being rude. Go over there and spend time with the traitor cats."

Drew smiled as he waited for the walking light to come on at an intersection. TJ might have come to Task Force Hawaii to investigate Charity for aiding a terrorist, but the two had fallen in love. They were perfect together.

"Well, do you know what you're going to wear?"

"A pair of dress pants and nice shirt. No graphic tees, I promise."

"Okay."

"Is there anything else you need from me, my Nubian princess?"

She chuckled at the nickname he had given her when she first came to Hawaii. "Nope. Just thought I would check up on you. I heard there is a connection with the other cases."

"Yeah, roses, notes."

He started walking again and wondered what Charity wanted. It wasn't like her to call for no reason other than to chit chat. Well, that was a lie. She did that, but he sensed there was something else she wanted to talk about. She rarely spent this long trying to come up with the courage to talk to him about something.

"How are things going with Cat?"

And there it was. "They're fine. We are keeping it cool right now."

Another snort.

"What?"

"There is nothing *cool* about you two. Both of you give each other hot looks when you think the other party isn't looking."

"We do not."

"Andrew Franklin, don't you lie to me or I will call your mama."

"Go right ahead, and then you can tell her about the case."

"Stop trying to change the subject. If you don't want to talk about it, just say butt out, Charity."

"Butt out, Charity."

"Fine. But just so you know, you don't have me fooled. I know you too well. Just let me know if you need to talk about it. You know I am always here for you."

He sighed. "I know."

"Be careful and call if you need help tomorrow night."

"Good lord. I know how to dress myself."

"That is up for debate."

"TJ is right. You're rude."

She chuckled. "Night, Drew."

"Night, Charity."

He clicked off the phone, wondering again why he had never been attracted to Charity. Other than the fact she wasn't attracted to him at all. It had been Cat. She had always been there in his mind, and he could never see another woman other than her. Plus, he sort of felt like a brother to Charity.

He entered the code to get into his building, and then went to the elevator. Before it arrived, a young businesswoman, white, with long blonde hair and a sexy smile stepped into the lobby. The door dinged and he held it open for her before stepping in.

"Thank you."

"No problem."

He pushed the button for his condo floor. He lived on the top floor.

She was going to three.

They rode in silence until they got to her floor. He had noted the fuck me heels and red power suit. No mistaking, in some kind of business, and not from Hawaii. Even business people on the islands dressed down, but for *haoles* from the mainland, they sometimes never learned. Even at this hour, her makeup was perfect, and he sensed she kept stealing glances at him with her big blue eyes. The doors opened and she started to walk out, but she put her hand out to hold the door open. She pulled a business card from her bag and handed it to Drew.

"If you're interested, give me a call."

Then she stepped out and walked away. He should be interested. She was the kind of woman who garnered attention from just about every heterosexual man around. But, instead, he felt absolutely fucking nothing.

One thing was for certain. He needed to get a life after they finished this investigation.

In the dark, not far from where Drew lived, someone sat obsessing. The only light came from the computer screen, which displayed pictures of Drew from the paper, and online. So sweet, so gorgeous. But men always looked that way before they disappointed you. *Always.*

She rocked back and forth in her chair and fixated on her newest possession. Soon, he would be hers.

# TANGLED PASSIONS

# CHAPTER TEN

Cat fought the urge to tap her foot, or bite her fingernails down to the nub. Nothing she did seemed to be able to calm her nerves. The four cups of coffee she'd had today probably didn't help either.

Most people would think it was the fact this was her first lead. But it wasn't, not entirely. No, this had more to do with the man now standing in the conference area with her. She knew he was smart, and he contributed to a lot of the cases, but she didn't like the idea of Drew acting as bait.

She decided to make sure to go back over the rules just one more time.

"Now, remember to keep your phone hidden so she doesn't see what is going on."

"I did this two days ago, Cat. I can handle it," he said as he slipped the earbud in, quiet irritation easy to hear in his voice.

Cat knew he was pissed at her. She didn't care. She wanted him safe and, for some reason, she worried that something would go wrong. It was a hunch, and her hunches were rarely wrong. But it was an easy job, one that they both could handle. Drew hadn't done much undercover work, but this should be easy enough. Still, every time she thought about him at dinner with a possible killer, it turned her stomach into a gelatinous bundle of nerves. She was glad that she hadn't eaten anything since breakfast. There was a good chance Drew would be wearing it by now.

"Are you ready?"

He nodded, then looked behind her. He smiled. "Hey, Emma."

She turned and saw Emma walk in with Del right behind her. He was holding baby Evie.

"Hey. Del had some work to do, so I thought I would keep Cat company while you went on your date, which I'm sure will be boring."

He laughed. "You crack me up, but I have to agree. Most first dates are boring."

She heard the way his voice changed over the sentence and she glanced at him. She couldn't tell what he was thinking, but her thoughts moved back to their one and only date. It had been at Emma and Del's wedding, the day before their lives had changed forever. It had been magical and wonderful, and then it wasn't.

She pushed that thought aside.

"I'm not even going to comment on that," Del said. "I'm off to do some paperwork. Here," he said, handing their baby to Emma. He kissed their little girl on the nose. "See you later, short stuff."

"I guess I should get going," Drew said.

"Remember, try to get info about Branson out of her, but don't push too much," Cat said.

"I know. Don't worry."

"When you get there, be sure to test the earbud. I want to make sure we have a good connection."

"Sure thing."

"If you think something is off, just get out of there. If she's the killer, she's killed without any remorse before, and we don't want you taking any stupid risks."

"I understand. I'm not stupid."

"Okay, sure."

Still, she had to resist giving him a hug before he went. Completely inappropriate, and not like her at all, but she so badly needed assurance that he would be okay.

"Anything else?" Drew asked. He was standing there looking completely fuckable, with a pair of black dress slacks and a red Hawaiian shirt.

"Cat?"

Yes, don't go.

"No. Just be careful."

And with a salute, he was off to his date. She watched him leave and heard Emma sigh behind her. It was one of those sighs that told Cat that Emma was bored.

"What?" she asked, not turning around. She could still see Drew as he walked to the front door of the building. She hoped he'd listened to her and that he didn't make any mistakes tonight.

"You two really need to work out your issues."

As soon as she could no longer see Drew, Cat turned to face Emma. "What do you mean?"

Emma rolled her eyes as she swayed back and forth to keep the baby quiet. "I've held my tongue for months, but you both look at each other as if you want to find the closest flat surface."

She blinked. "I do not."

Emma snorted. "Bollocks."

"And he does not. In fact, he's made it very clear that nothing will ever happen."

Just saying the words physically hurt her. She had accepted his feelings on the subject months ago, but she still hadn't gotten over it. The fact that it was her fault entirely wasn't easy to deal with either.

"Double bollocks."

"Is that even a thing?" she asked.

"Don't try to change the subject. You are both hung up on each other. Everyone is talking about it. Taking bets even."

"On what?"

"When you both will finally give in to your need for a good, hard shag."

She closed her eyes and tried to forget she even heard what Emma had just said. She didn't want people to pity her because she was so hung up on Drew.

"Oh, don't do that," Emma said, disgust threading her voice.

Cat opened her eyes. "What?"

"God, you Americans." Emma was English by birth, and spent most of her life in Thailand before moving to Hawaii. "You use sex to sell everything, but you're so puritanical about your own sex lives. Good sex is healthy. Normal."

"It's not that."

"Then what?"

She shrugged.

"Bloody hell, Cat. Just spit it out. God, I thought I was bad."

Cat chuckled. "Normally you are a little too blunt."

Emma just stared at her. She wasn't just smart; she was a genius. Knowing Emma, she could easily join Mensa, but wouldn't because she had issues. Still, because of her intellect, Cat understood there was little she could do to hide her feelings. When she still said nothing, she knew Emma was waiting for an answer, and there was a good chance she would not go away until she got it.

"Okay." She sighed. "I hate thinking people pity me because I'm hung up on Drew."

Emma snorted. "You're hung up on each other. That is not one-sided."

"He *was*. Not sure he still is."

"Yeah, sure. That's why he almost melts when you are up there talking at the briefings."

Her heart skipped a beat. "He does not."

"Charity said he practically drooled all over her when you were giving a briefing."

She opened her mouth, then snapped it shut. Had she

really misread all the signals? No, he had shut her down just a few months ago. He had said that he didn't want to even be friends anymore. She'd had her chance and she had wrecked it. Until now, she thought she had come to terms with it.

"I know you have some craziness going on in your brain," Emma said as she patted Evie's back. "But I just say wait and see. Plus, don't wait too long because I have a bet for this week."

Cat frowned. "When?"

"Can't tell. That's a new rule Charity instituted."

Good lord, they were going to need a manual for all their betting rules. "I'm also worried about him. He's never done anything like this."

Emma shook her head. "Everyone thinks he's weak, but he isn't."

"Not weak. He's inexperienced."

"But smart. Very smart. Don't worry. Drew will be able to handle the mission."

She opened her mouth to argue, but Emma interrupted her. "Let's get some munchies before this starts, and you can argue with me later."

Cat wanted to refuse, but she'd only had breakfast, so she agreed.

"I think there are even some leftover malasadas in the break room," Cat said.

"No. I need a real dinner. Let's order a pizza. I've been craving a good, greasy pizza."

Cat smiled. "That sounds good."

"I'll order. You don't like onions or peppers, right?"

Cat nodded.

"Be right back." She watched Emma hurry off to Del's office with Evie in her arms. She might not have solved her problems or worries, but talking things over with Emma put her mind at ease, at least a little bit.

She decided to do the monitoring in the conference area because it had more room. Sitting down, she resolved to push her worries aside and just work on the surveillance. She'd worry about her own feelings later. This case was too important.

Drew followed Lana Cho to their table. As per their agreement, they had met in front of the restaurant he had chosen. He'd gone for one of the chains, wanting to avoid any of the locally owned dining choices. If Hawaii was small and everyone knew each other, his family and those who worked and owned their own restaurants, was microscopic. Everyone knew everyone else, and they all knew his family for sure. He'd end up getting a call from his mother before the date had ended.

He smiled at Lana as he waited for her to take her seat before taking his. After the waiter gave him the specials and took their drink and appetizer orders, he hurried off. Drew was glad that Charity had suggested he make reservations. It had been late in the day on Friday when he'd called, but he had been able to get them a table at seven for Saturday

"I know you probably hear this a lot, but I've been to your family's restaurants," Lana said as she peered over the massive menu.

She was a tiny woman, just over five feet tall and probably weighed no more than ninety pounds. In her bio, Asian, with short hair that stopped right at her chin, and green eyes; she hadn't changed much since she'd had the photo taken listed on her bio page. Her tastes appeared to run expensive, from her designer clothes to the tennis bracelet that had to be at least five carats. She might just be a simple phlebotomist, but she had to have family money to afford those kinds of things.

"I don't think there is anyone who hasn't," he said. "Did you grow up on Oahu?"

A tiny ping of guilt stabbed at his conscious. He knew this was part of the job, but it didn't make him feel any less a jerk for asking questions. Cat had given him a pretty extensive write up on Lana and her background, so he knew most of the chit chat type of conversation.

"No. I grew up on Maui. Most of my family still lives there."

"Must be nice. My family is always in my hair."

She shook her head. "I thought it would be, but I get kind of homesick every now and then."

"Something only kama'āina would understand, yeah?"

She smiled. It was sweet, and her green eyes danced with humor. Yep, he was going to hell. "Yeah. So, do you know what is good here?"

"All the grilled fish is great."

She looked over the menu, and by the time the waiter came back over, they were both ready to order.

"You work for Task Force Hawaii, then?"

"In a way. I work for the medical examiner, who works for them. I'm her assistant."

"Cool. I always thought that would be an interesting job. Do you get to do a lot of testing and stuff?"

He shook his head. "No. That's our forensics tech. I assist in autopsies and help with reports."

"Do you have a medical degree?"

"No. I'm taking a few classes here and there so I can get it done, but I'm in no rush. I enjoy my work."

She nodded. "I get that question all the time too. I mean, I love being a phlebotomist. I guess you could say it is in my blood...so to speak."

He chuckled. "Good one. Where do you work?"

"In Aiea; although, I would rather work on the windward side. I want to move other there."

"I hear ya. I won't ever get that choice, but I like the idea of living over there too. I grew up there."

"Yeah?"

He nodded. "Most of my family lives over there. It's

funny because we have people in our office who have moved halfway across the world, but my parents act like I have committed a sin by living in Honolulu."

She laughed as their waiter brought their appetizers. They both took healthy portions of the poke before she responded.

"Yes. When I told my parents I was moving here, they acted as if I said I wanted to be a serial killer."

A chill washed over Drew. He looked up at that comment and stopped for a long moment. She was smiling as if it were a joke, but he wasn't sure. He knew that sociopaths loved to do things like that. Make jokes, even while knowing they were doing just that.

"So, how long have you been using Premiere Connections?" she asked.

"You're my first date."

Her eyes widened. "No."

"Yep," he said with a smile. "I heard about them through an investigation. Plus, I heard they were really good."

"An investigation?" she asked.

"Branson Anderson. We're investigating his death."

"Oh?" she asked, her smile fading.

"Yeah. I have nothing to do with that part of the investigation. Just all body work. My work is done, but they brought back information on Premiere Connections, so I thought I would check them out. "

"I dated him, you know?"

"Who? Branson?"

She nodded. "He was nice, but, he wasn't right for me. A little too old."

He wanted to ask her why she went out with him three times then, but he held his tongue.

"What was he like? I saw him speak once at my school, but I never personally met him."

"He was a complete workaholic. It was hard to get time together when he had his ear attached to his phone. I found it all boring. Other than that, he was nice. It was a waste of time though."

"What was?"

"The dates. They were a waste of time."

"Why do you say that?"

She hesitated, and he realized he might have stepped over a boundary.

"I'm sorry. That was personal."

"No, I brought it up and it was no secret. He was still in love with his wife. Easy to see. Kind of sad, but sweet in a way. To find someone you loved that much...I guess that's all anyone can hope for."

He smiled. "Definitely."

She took a sip of wine and watched him over the rim of the glass.

"So, how long have you been using Premiere Connections?" he asked.

"A few years. I'm not always current, and I've only dated a handful of guys."

"Ah. Are you telling me you're selective, because I might get a big head?"

She laughed. "I might be doing just that, Mr. Drew Franklin."

"I feel kind of honored."

"You should."

She was smiling at him, and her eyes were still dancing with amusement, and not for the first time that night, he felt like a total ass. He had to stop that. He wasn't being horrible, and truth was, if they found nothing else on Lana, she would never know she was investigated. If she was the killer, it was best that they had this information ahead of their interview.

"Okay, tell me why you like to play with blood?" he asked, wishing that this date would end as soon as possible.

# TANGLED PASSIONS

# CHAPTER ELEVEN

By the end of the night, Drew was sure Lana wasn't the killer. Not that he was skilled at investigation, but he was a good judge of human nature. It was the one thing that had allowed him to escape most of the nerd beatings his friends had been victim to.

"I really had a good time tonight," Lana said as they stopped by her car. "God, that sounded lame."

"Not lame. I had a good time too."

She smiled. "That's good."

He knew what she was expecting, and normally he would just say goodnight and walk away. The problem was that he had to appear to be dating the women. His other issue was that he knew he had an audience. How did undercover cops handle this?

He stepped closer, placed a hand on one hip, then lowered his mouth to hers. One soft kiss and he knew. No spark, nothing. There was no excitement, at least on his part. He pulled back and dropped his hand. Lana's eyes fluttered open, and it was easy to see that maybe he wasn't interested, but she clearly was.

"I'll give you a call."

She shook her head. "You don't have to say that, Drew."

"No. I will."

She gave him a shy smile and then got into her Honda, and he watched her drive away. For a long moment, he stood there, wondering about the night. He hadn't dated since before the shooting. After tonight, he might just take a chance on it again. At least when this case was done.

He walked back to his car and started on his way to return to TFH. It had been difficult to ignore the fact that everyone had been listening. New dates were bad enough, but dealing with a whole horde of folks listening in wasn't that much fun. Add in that they were now recording the exchange, and if they picked up on anything, it would be entered in to evidence. It could be played in court.

With a sigh, he pushed that thought out of his head and drove the back streets to TFH. He parked his car in the rear. For a long moment, he sat there and looked at the back entrance. Close to a year ago, his whole life had changed. One little mistake, one little bullet, and everything had gone to shit. A man bent on hurting Elle had lost control and a stray shot had hit him. He and Cat had just had one memorable night together. He would never be able to forget that.

The first day back had been the worst, but now, it was just a dull ache every now and then. That's why the last few days had been horrific for him. Facing her every now and then wasn't that bad, and their paths only crossed at briefings or the occasional team get together. Now though, they had to spend time together for the case. Getting ready had been bad enough, but going over evidence was going to be worse. Like when he had to talk to her about a date he'd just been on. He scrubbed a hand over his face trying to clear his head before going into the building. When he felt ready, he stepped out of his car and headed for the door. He walked down the hallway and then up the stairs to the first floor.

The place was dark and deserted. Light spilled out from Cat's office, telling him that she was still there. He walked quietly to her doorway and then stood there and stared at her. He rarely got time alone with her anymore, and most of that was by his own design.

"I thought there would be more people."

She turned around, seemingly out of breath. "Damn, I didn't hear you."

"Hmm." There was something so damned sexy about a breathless Cat.

"Where is everyone?" he asked.

"Emma and the boss went home. Evie was a little fussy. Graeme was in for a while. Elle apparently has been going to sleep around eight at night."

He smiled. "That's good."

The silence stretched out and he waited for her to say something, anything. But she didn't. He realized that unless he said something, they could be stuck there all night. He handed her the earbud and the tracking device. "Here you go. It was hard to act casually."

"You didn't seem to have a problem," she said as she stored the earbud and GPS devices in her desk drawer.

He frowned. "What's that supposed to mean?"

"Just that. You were good tonight."

"Oh, don't kill me with your praise." She didn't smile like he had hoped. "Cat, what you said. What did it mean?"

"Nothing."

"No, it meant something."

She sighed. "Just go, Drew."

He wanted to do just that, but his instincts told him to push the discussion.

"No, I think you need to tell me what you really meant by that."

"I said just go. I don't want to talk about it. It seemed like a really nice date, and you appeared to like her."

Was that jealousy he heard? No, it couldn't be. She didn't have feelings for him, or she wouldn't have given him the brushoff when he had been shot. People who cared stuck around. Still, she had been acting strangely, but maybe it was because they were working on the case together. He couldn't say he was all that comfortable with the situation, and he knew she couldn't be either.

He opened his mouth to say something else, but she ignored him.

"Make sure to contact those other three women."

It sounded like a normal order, but beneath the surface, he detected a thread of irritation.

"I will."

"Fine."

He turned to leave, then stopped. "Are you sure there's nothing wrong?"

Her back was to him, but he could see her reflection in the computer screen. She closed her eyes and seemed to pray for patience. "Yes."

"Good night."

She waved her hand as if it were too much for her to answer him. He walked out of her office, irritated and still not sure what he did wrong. But there is one thing he had learned in the last year: trying to figure out Catherine Kalakau was just a waste of energy and time.

For as long as Cat could remember, early Sunday mornings meant Liliha coco puffs and then church. She rarely made it to her mother's house on Sundays, and today would be no different. It wasn't that she hated her mother. She loved her. And that was why she had to stay away. Every time they were together, there seemed to be an argument and for some reason, Sundays seemed to be worse than any other day of the week.

She sat on her surfboard and looked out over the water. The area was dotted with surfers waiting for the next wave. It wasn't all that good of a surfing day, but she had to get out of her house. Looking over the files was starting to get to her. Add in the fact that she felt guilty for being rude to Drew last night, and she really didn't want to be in a confined space.

Her father had always said the one place he found peace was on the water.

Water is life.

He said it all the time. So, she'd grabbed her board and headed out.

And, she had found some peace. There was something about hearing the water lap against her surfboard. It soothed her.

It also made her think.

She was going to have to fix this situation with Drew. They needed to move on so they could work together. There was always a chance that he would end up working with her on other cases. They couldn't deal with this constant nastiness...most of it coming from her.

She didn't want to talk to him in the office. Instead, she decided to pop over to his apartment later today. The sooner they got it all cleared away, the easier it would be at the office.

As she heard the rush of the next wave, she laid down on her board to prepare for it. For now, this was all she needed to make her feel whole.

Drew had an early morning for Sunday. He'd promised his mother he would make it to church and a Sunday lunch. He had done both and gotten stuck talking to them—or rather, avoiding the conversation about—the case. After a run on the beach and a shower, Drew decided he was owed a night off.

He'd just stretched out on the couch to catch up on TV, when his doorbell rang around five. He walked to the door, a sense of foreboding weighing on his shoulders. He had a feeling he knew who was on the other side of the door.

He looked through the peephole and almost groaned when he saw Cat. The woman was trying to kill him. He was sure of it. The night before, he had been plagued with dreams about her. Hot, sweaty dreams that had left him aroused and irritated. It had been months since that had happened, but he assumed it was because they were working together. He wanted this damned case cleared as soon as possible. Otherwise, he might just die from lack of blood to his brain.

He opened the door.

"Hey."

She wasn't smiling, but Cat hadn't been smiling much lately. "Hey. Do you mind if come in?"

*Yes.* "No."

He stepped back and let her pass. The sweet scent of her tickled his senses. Just that had his body humming. He shut the door and followed her in. Damn, she was wearing board shorts. That, along with the little blue tank top, had his fingers itching to touch.

"Is there something new with the case?"

She stopped in the kitchen and turned to face him. She looked so unsure of herself, so unlike the woman he knew.

She licked her lips, then said, "No. Well, sort of. I wanted to apologize."

"For what?"

"For being kind of nasty last night. There was no call for it, and it was unprofessional."

"Okay. I don't think you were that nasty, but I accept."

She studied him for a long minute. "Just like that?"

"Yeah, just like that."

"Fine."

The curt response tugged a smile from his lips. She had been a little bothered by it. She wouldn't be so rude if not. "There's that word again."

She rolled her eyes and raked her hand through her long black hair. He followed the movement, he couldn't help it. He knew how soft her hair was. It had brushed against his cheek when they had kissed last year.

Dammit.

"Sorry. I just…it won't happen again."

She was fidgeting. Cat never fidgeted. In fact, she was known to have nerves of steel. He knew that it was one of her tells. When they were playing cards, Adam had told him to watch the other players, observe their behavior. Even when Cat was nervous, she would stay still.

"I wasn't that upset about it."

But the mere thought that she might be jealous had occupied his thoughts and, apparently, influenced his dreams.

"Cool. Well, I'll get going.'

But she didn't move.

"I will let it go if you can tell me one thing."

"What?" she asked, crossing her arms beneath her breasts.

He cocked his head to the side and watched her. Oh, yes, she was irritated, and she wanted to be anywhere but there. It was easy to see. "Why did you get so mad?"

"I don't like you having to do this job. You're a civilian, and there is no reason for you to be involved."

"I think there is. But I don't think you're telling me the truth."

Her eyes narrowed as he took a step closer. God, there was that scent again. Every now and then, he would catch a whiff of it at the office. It wasn't perfume. Cat didn't like that stuff. No, this was pure Cat. Soft, subtle, with a mere hint of spice from the herbal soap she used. It was so hard not to want to take a big, luscious bite.

"And what do you think the reason is?"

"You were jealous of Lana."

She snorted. "Not likely."

That snort, along with the unsteadiness of her voice,

told him she was lying. He stepped closer, crowding her against the kitchen counter. "Oh, yeah. You were."

She lifted her chin. "Damn cocky to think that way, if you ask me."

He shook his head as he leaned down. He could feel the heat of her body. They were mere inches apart.

"Maybe. But, I'm right."

"No." Her voice quivered when she spoke.

He nodded. "And you know what the most embarrassing thing is?"

She shook her head as her tongue darted out over her fuller, bottom lip.

"It's kind of a turn on. It shouldn't be, but it is."

"Drew..." her voice trailed off as he leaned closer still.

He knew it was now or never. He had spent so much time trying to romance her last time. Months of preparation, all carefully orchestrated. This time, though, it was different. He wanted all that romance, but the only thought that consumed him was having...*her*. Right now. That one thought pulsed through his blood. The need to take, to conquer, it was all he cared about. He needed her on a level that he just didn't even understand himself. So, to make sure he never had any regrets about Cat, he bent his head and kissed her.

The first taste was exhilarating. It was as wonderful as he remembered. He started to fall, right there and then. He knew it was probably stupid, idiotic after what happened last time. His body and heart didn't care.

Before he lost control, he pulled back and looked down at her. She opened her eyes and looked up at him. Desire shimmered in her gaze. It was then that he knew he had her.

"Your choice. Yes or no?"

Her tongue darted out again, and he followed the motion with is eyes. Then he raised his gaze to meet hers. It was still there, the need...she wanted him. She could deny him, but something shifted over her expression that he couldn't discern.

"Yes."

"Thank God," he said before slamming his mouth down on hers and losing himself in her.

# TANGLED PASSIONS

# CHAPTER TWELVE

Searing heat spiraled through Cat's veins as Drew slanted his mouth over hers and deepened the kiss. She could do nothing else, other than surrender to the passion. It crashed over her and through her entire being.

He pulled back from the kiss and she felt lost.

"Cat. Look at me."

His voice ground out and she did as he ordered. This was not the sweet man who had stolen kisses. This was a stranger, one that excited and scared her simultaneously. His dark brown eyes seemed almost darker, somehow possessed. He wanted something, and she was the thing that he wanted. He stepped closer and slipped his hands around her waist. With one hard yank, he pulled her against him. Her heartbeat was out of control.

"If you're just fucking around with me, you better tell me right now," he said, biting out every word so it felt like a hammer to her soul. "You can save any little shred of civility we have between us."

She opened her mouth, but he stopped her by shaking

his head.

"But, if you say yes now, just know there will be no pretending it didn't happen later. I won't go back to being your little buddy you pat on the head. You might not want to go on after this, but one thing is for sure, I'm not going to be in that *friend* category anymore."

She should say no. It would be the smart thing to do. Their lives were complicated and right now, they had other things to worry about. He would want more than she thought she was capable of giving him. Drew would demand more than just a little fun in bed. Cat knew she wasn't good enough for him...for anyone. But in this one moment, in this split second, she yearned. She wanted to be good enough, to be the woman he thought she was. So, instead of saying no, or stepping away, she cupped his face. Rising up on her toes, she didn't hesitate. Instead, she pressed her lips against his, opening her mouth immediately. He stole inside, tangling his tongue against hers. She wrapped her arms around his neck and pressed against him. Her head spun, any objection she could have come up with dissolved as he deepened the kiss and took complete control.

He walked her backwards as he continued to kiss her. When her back hit the wall, he pulled back. He rubbed his thumb over her mouth, his gaze completely focused on the action. She slipped her tongue out, teasing the tip of his finger. Heat flared in the depths of his gaze as he slid his index finger between her lips. She sucked on it, then wrapped her tongue around the digit. He groaned, yanked it out of her mouth so he could kiss her. This kiss wasn't as calculated. It was hot and wet and exhilarating. By the time he pulled back, she felt as if the whole world was spinning around them.

Without a word, he grabbed the bottom of her shirt and pulled it off over her head. He made quick work of her bra, tossing it on the floor behind him. As he looked at her, he said nothing. She was a woman who had fought against the stereotype that told her she was too flat chested, too…boyish. It was something boys had teased her about for years…now, even men did.

His gaze locked on her breasts as he raised a hand and skimmed her nipple with the back of his knuckles. Barely a touch, but it tightened immediately…painfully. She sucked in a breath.

"Beautiful," he said, in the barest of whispers. He leaned closer and touched the tip with his tongue, teasing it, then laying the flat of his tongue against it.

Oh, God, he was undoing her with the small touches, the teasing…her entire body was ready to explode—and she still had her pants on. He moved on to her other breast, scraping his teeth over the nipple. The movement, along with the way he teased and pinched her other nipple, shot straight to her sex. Before she was ready, he was moving away to drop to his knees. He kissed her stomach on the way down, before unbuttoning, then unzipping her pants. He skimmed them down her legs, and she thought, once again, that maybe she should invest in some sexier lingerie. Plain cotton was her choice, especially on the job, but apparently, Drew could care less. He pressed his mouth against the simple fabric. Wet heat flooded her pussy before he moved away.

She stepped out of her pants, then he did the same with her panties. And now she stood in front of him, completely naked. He skimmed his hands up her legs, to her hips, his fingers dancing over her flesh. She had always thought he had the most amazing hands. Long fingered…a pianist's hands. There were times she would be watching as he worked on the keyboard, his clever digits flying over the keys. Now, they slipped over her skin.

He leaned forward and drew in a deep breath. It was one of the most intimate things any man had ever done to her—and the most erotic. He gave her no time to even come to terms with that. The first touch of his tongue against her sex almost had her coming right then and there. It was silly to even contemplate an orgasm with barely any foreplay, but Drew apparently knew exactly what she wanted... *needed.*

His tongue ran along her slit, then slipped inside of her. As he tasted her, his fingers were now digging into her flesh, but she could care less. Over and over, he dove into her sex. He added one finger, as he pulled her clit between his teeth. Her knees buckled and she almost fell, but he held her there, trapped against his sensual assault. Simple sexual hunger transformed into a craving that took over her entire body. She squirmed against his mouth, but he would give her no relief. Instead, he held her in place, not allowing her to move, to take control. Moving his mouth away, he added another finger and pressed his thumb against her clit. Over and over, he teased her. She struggled still, trying to gain control over his sensual assault, but he did not give her the chance. In fact, every time she attempted to thwart his own control over the situation, he punished her by slowing down his rhythm.

Just as she felt her orgasm approaching, thinking that this time she would reach completion, he pulled back and away from her. She almost toppled over on him, but he held her steady as he rose to his feet. He kissed her then, and if she thought the first kiss knocked her off balance, this one was far more powerful. She could taste herself on his lips as he cupped her face in his hands and deepened the kiss. Every nerve in her body felt as if it were on fire, her entire focus on the feel of his tongue as it danced over her own. Now, all she could think about was him, this moment, and the way he made her feel.

He pulled back, and she shivered as cold air washed over her. As she opened her eyes, she found him watching her. Fierce hunger darkened his eyes as his gaze moved down her body then back up. Before she knew what he was doing, he lifted her into his arms and carried her to the couch. He set her down, then tugged off his t-shirt, throwing it behind him. She saw it then, the scar that marred the almost perfect golden brown skin.

Drew leaned down to kiss her, but she stopped him by putting her hand on his chest. She slipped her fingers over the damaged skin. She bent her head and pressed her mouth against the hard ridges. Opening her mouth, she slid her tongue over them. Drew shuddered against her.

"Cat."

She looked up and found herself trapped by his dark gaze. He held her face and leaned down to kiss her. At first, it was just a brush of his mouth over hers. Soft, fleeting, tempting. Then, he skimmed the tip of his tongue against the seam of her lips. Cat did not hesitate, not this time, or probably ever again. She was captured by this man, the one who made her laugh, and the one who inspired a craving that she would never be able to ignore. She opened her mouth and he stole inside.

His hands slipped down her back to her ass. Those talented fingers pressed into her flesh, urging her closer. She shuddered against him, her body ready for release. She wanted to feel his skin—all of it. She slipped her hands down to the waistband of his jeans. Without breaking the kiss, she undid the button and unzipped them.

She wrapped her hand around his cock and stroked him. He broke away from the kiss and groaned, letting his head fall back. As she continued to tease him, she kissed his neck, tasting the salty sweetness of his flesh, dragging her tongue over his Adam's apple. He swallowed, as she continued to stroke him. Power surged through her as she tested his control. It surged through her, along with another wave of arousal that blinded her to everything but this man…this moment.

She rose to her tiptoes once more to brush her mouth against his. When she finished, she looked up at his expression.

"You're playing with fire, Cat."

She smiled as she gave his shaft a leisurely stroke. "I've always preferred heat to cold."

Drew groaned. "I should have known you would test my limits, woman."

He didn't wait for her to respond. Instead, he stepped out of his jeans, then turned them around, falling onto the couch. With a tug, he urged her closer. She straddled his hips. She leaned down for another kiss before she rose to her knees. Slowly, she lowered herself onto his cock. Finally, the connection she had craved for so long. Her nerve endings were already overly sensitive from his teasing, but it added to the complexity of her emotions. She was quivering by the time she had him fully embedded. Placing her hands on the couch behind him, she leaned forward to give him a kiss. Then, she started to move. At first, she took it slowly. She wanted to make this last. She had been waiting so long for this to happen. Cat refused to change the momentum as she continued. Drew had been the one in charge, building the delicious hunger that now controlled her every thought.

Soon though, she was ensnared in a web of her own making. Her body demanded satisfaction. Cat felt her orgasm approaching and started to increase her rhythm. Drew wasn't having that. He pulled her closer and latched his mouth onto her nipple. By doing so, he kept her trapped, unable to move. Her entire being was a pulsing hormone, ready for release, but he apparently didn't care.

"Drew," she said.

He glanced up at her, then without breaking eye contact, he took her other nipple into his mouth. He held her there, his ardent gaze never wavering from hers. Just that look sent another surge of lust scorching through her. She wanted to move, but Drew held her still, his hands on her hips. She was so close to her release that she was shaking with need. Drew continued to take his time, as if there was no great rush. Frustration welled up inside of her, and she decided to act. She couldn't move up and down, but she could move her hips. The small movement sent a wave of shocked heat racing through her

133

bloodstream. Even better, it pulled a moan from Drew. He closed his eyes and sucked harder on her nipple. The sweet tension only had her more determined. She twisted her hips again, and he dug his fingers into her flesh.

Power surged through her now that she knew she was getting to him. She made the small move again, then again. Soon, he pulled back from her breasts and groaned, his head falling to the back of the couch. Renewed with a sense of purpose, she started to move again, and this time she did not slow down. And just when she thought relief was so far off, she felt her orgasm approaching once again. She did not relent in her pursuit.

Drew had given her the control, and she took full advantage of it. Leaning down, she took his mouth in a hot, wet kiss; sucking on his tongue as she increased her rhythm. When she pulled back, she watched as pleasure washed over him, his orgasm shuttering through him as she continued to ride him. He opened his eyes and looked at her.

"Come with me, Cat."

She couldn't resist. Not now—not ever. Cat let her head fall back as a powerful release slammed through her, so intense, it almost stole her breath. She writhed against him as it crashed over her. Drew slipped his hands up her body to her head, as he urged her to lean down. He kissed her then, and she couldn't ignore the connection. In that one moment, she knew she had never had an experience like this, and probably never would again, at least not with another man.

When they pulled back from the kiss, they were both breathless. She collapsed against him, her head on his shoulder. She should probably worry that they were working a case and this was highly inappropriate. Later, she promised herself. That is when she would think about all their issues. Right now, she just wanted this, to be here in his arms and know that in this one space of time, they were connected.

It was her last thought before she drifted off to sleep.

# CHAPTER THIRTEEN

The trade winds shifted, blowing through Drew's apartment and waking him up. It took a moment or two for him to come to terms with his situation. Cat was still sitting on top of him, and they were on the couch. As the cooler air filled the room, he felt her shiver, although she didn't wake up. Instead, she tightened her hold.

Drew kissed her temple, then looked out the massive floor-to-ceiling windows. The drapes danced on the breeze that flowed through the opening and then it hit him: the fucking drapes were open. Damn. He was lucky his condo was on the top floor and, hopefully, no one saw them.

"Hey," he said.

Cat grumbled and snuggled closer. He smiled. Her breath was against his neck and her hair was sliding over his shoulder. His brain was still mushy, unable to think beyond the here and now. Of course, he didn't give a shit about anything else. She was in his arms, and he had done his damnedest to claim her. Still, they should probably get up and go to the bedroom. Knowing his luck, there would be some kind of aerial photography going on.

"Cat."

"Go away."

He chuckled and decided to get them into the bedroom himself. He slipped his hands beneath her rear end, then stood up. They swayed, but he steadied them. Damn, he was wiped out.

"What are you doing?" she asked, even as she settled her head on his shoulder.

"Taking us to the bedroom."

"M'okay."

He shook his head and walked into his bedroom. After laying her on the bed, he went into the bathroom, cleaned up, and then joined her back in the bedroom. When he reached his bed, he stood there, unable to still grasp what had happened. Catherine Kalakau was in his bed. She had just melted his brain, seared her ownership over his heart, and now she was apparently spending the night.

After what had happened last year, he didn't think this would ever happen. Now, though, it was still hard to fathom.

What did it mean and where did they go from here?

Drew had no idea what the future held for them. He wanted more. Hell, he wanted the whole thing. Her rejection had been more painful that the fucking bullet he took. Now, he wanted some sort of agreement of something. He wanted to know she wasn't going to rush out the door and then pretend nothing happened. One thing was certain, he would never figure it out standing here staring at her. It was kind of creepy and if someone saw him, there is good chance they'd call the police. He decided to join her in bed. It took him some maneuvering, but he got them both under the sheet.

"I guess we're going to have to talk about this," she said.

"Not necessarily."

She lifted her head up and looked at him. "Yeah, we do. That's why it got all screwed up to begin with.

"Okay. But first, we need to address the elephant in the room."

"That this is wholly inappropriate in the middle of an investigation?"

He chuckled. "That seems about par for our office,

considering how everyone seems to be hooking up."

"Then what?"

"We didn't use protection. I didn't even think of it."

Her mouth formed an "o". She shook her head. "I'm on the pill, and I haven't been active since my last physical."

"And I haven't since the accident."

"You mean since you were shot, you haven't been with anyone?"

He shook his head. "I couldn't for a long time because the doctors were worried. After that, I just haven't wanted to get out there. So, you want to talk about us? About what happened before?

She sighed. "If you don't want to, we don't have to."

"I said okay, didn't I?" he asked as he started toying with her hair. God, he loved it. It was so soft and silky. He liked the way it slipped through his fingers. The sweet scent of her shampoo was always a hidden pleasure for him.

"If you're mad—"

He tugged playfully on a few strands.

"I'm not mad. I just said that if you want to talk, we can. Although, I will warn you, my brain is slow. Very slow right now."

She frowned in a completely not Cat looking way. In fact, there was a bit of a pout with it. Pouting wasn't something that he normally associated with Cat. She was so damned cute. Of course, if he told her, she would probably break his nose, then punch him in the nuts.

"What are you talking about?"

He studied her. "Are you fishing for a compliment?"

She stared at him for a long time, and he realized that she had no notion of what he was talking about. She truly didn't understand what she was to him, or how she affected him. He had never hidden how he felt about her, so it was odd that she really didn't realize what he was talking about.

138

"You blew my mind, woman. I can barely think straight."

Another beat of silence went by before a small smile curved her lips. "Yeah?"

He rolled his eyes. "Seriously, you have no idea?"

She shook her head. "I just thought it was me."

"You?"

"It's hard for me to describe, but I have never been taken like that. No one has ever made me feel the way you did."

He wanted to crow about that one little nugget, but along with it came a revelation. She felt the same way, that the lovemaking had been as amazing to her as it was to him. And that meant she could fall in love with him. Or she was in love with him, but didn't realize it. Either way, he decided to keep that information to himself.

"Okay, tell me what we need to talk about?"

She opened her mouth, then snapped it shut. She wasn't a woman who shared her feelings easily. Still, the idea that she was holding back now, irritated him.

"You wanted to talk about this, so you either talk about it or leave it the way it is."

She sighed. "It is difficult for me to talk about."

He felt the inevitable softening. It was always there for Cat, who constantly portrayed herself to be the tough woman. He knew for her family, she had to do that. But right now, with him, she had to understand that he wouldn't judge her.

"I know, but you started this."

"I...when you were shot, I didn't know how to handle it."

He said nothing; although, the need to smooth things over danced on the tip of his tongue. He could see how much this was bothering her, and he wanted to soothe her. But Cat was right. They needed to figure out what went wrong and where they would go from here.

"I ran, like a coward, then I blamed it on the situation."

"You said it was your fault."

"It *was* my fault. I sent you there to pick up the files for me. Otherwise, you wouldn't have gotten shot."

"We've been over this, Cat. If I hadn't been there, there is a good chance Elle would be dead."

"You don't know that."

"What I do know is that Stan Remington was the man with the gun. He's the one who shot me. If I hadn't been there, he might have hurt Elle. He was deranged. So, it isn't your fault. It's his."

She didn't say anything, and he realized that he was nearly shouting by the time he had finished speaking.

"I'm sorry, but I hate that you blame yourself."

"I have another confession to make."

"What?"

She hesitated, then said, "It wasn't that I felt guilty. I mean, I did, but there was something else that scared the living hell out of me."

He blinked at the vehemence in her voice. "What?"

"Losing you."

No hesitation this time. The truth…finally.

"Losing me? That's why you walked away? Why you ignored me while I was recovering?"

"I know. It makes me a coward, and it made me hate myself. I just…I've lost so many people I cared about, and I was just beginning to fall for you. I couldn't handle it. I took the cowardly way out and broke things off."

"Then why didn't you just do that? You could have come in and said that you didn't want to see me anymore. That would have been better than months of nothing from you; not really knowing what was going on."

"Because I *am* a coward, deep down," she said, her voice small. "When it comes to relationships, I have never had a healthy one. And…"

She trailed off, and he knew that she was avoiding something. What, he wasn't sure, but it was something big.

"What?" he urged.

"I knew if I faced the issue and told you, that I wouldn't last. That I would cave."

He heard the shame in her voice. Tears now spilled down her cheeks. This was a side of Cat he knew was there, but had never seen.

"Cave?"

She nodded and sniffed. "I couldn't handle you being hurt. It…it almost broke me, Drew. I thought, if I stayed away and put you in that friend zone again, that it would all go back to normal."

"But it didn't." he murmured. He took hold of her hand and threaded his fingers through hers.

"No."

He raised her hand to his lips and brushed her fingers with his mouth. "And how did that feel?"

"Like hell. It…it's hard to explain. If I thought you being shot was bad, seeing you every day and not being able to be part of your life was gut wrenching. It physically hurt."

He let the words sink in, then he felt his mouth curve. Damn if the woman didn't please him. The odd thing was that she thought she was a coward, but she was far from it. He knew it was a knee-jerk reaction she used to protect herself.

"You think this is funny?" she asked, her tone filled with equal parts anger and pain. She tried to pull her hand away from his, but he refused to let go. Instead, he gave her a gentle tug and she tumbled onto his chest.

"I don't think it is funny, but it does make me happy."

She opened her mouth to argue, but he silenced her with a kiss. When he pulled back, she was breathless.

"Why does it make you happy?"

He touched her face, the evidence of her tears was still there on her cheeks. Cat wasn't a woman who cried easily, or at the drop of a hat. It took a lot to get to her.

"Because I was miserable all the time too. I thought I was pathetic."

She shook her head. "Never."

"Then I have to say the same thing about you being a coward."

"But I was. I walked away from you when you almost died."

"No, you were trying to protect yourself."

"Yes. And that makes me—"

He placed a couple fingers on her lips. "Don't say it. It wasn't a shining moment for either of us, but I understand."

"How?" she asked against his fingers.

"I see you get ready to go out to work in the streets almost every day at work. What you do is important, but it is always dangerous. I know the rates of injuries on the job for cops. Every day, I watch you walk out, and I worry if it will be the last time that I see you. That some bastard won't shoot you or you'll end up risking your life for other people. It doesn't make either of us cowards."

She sighed.

"Dammit, out with it, woman."

"I walked away. When you needed me. I understand what you are saying, and I completely agree with it. But you didn't walk away."

In that moment, it would be so easy just to let her take the fall, to let her keep on believing that she was more at fault than him. He couldn't think. Not when he realized that this could be the start of a new relationship for them.

"Yeah, I did. I could have fought for us. I could have forced you to explain yourself, but it was better to bury all that, because I was afraid. I didn't want to lose you a second time."

Her eyes softened. "Drew."

"I couldn't handle it, not then, and not now. Just know that I'm going to be fighting like hell to keep you with me. There will be no letting you walk away."

Her mouth curved, and he felt it all the way to the soles of his feet. "Yeah?"

He nodded as she lifted herself up, then started sliding down his body. First there was a kiss, a nip, then the glide of her tongue against his flesh. She knelt between his legs and wrapped her hand around his cock. He was already rigid, a drop of precum wetting the head of it.

She didn't look down at his cock as she stroked him. No, she didn't break eye contact. Over and over, she slipped her hand over his hardened flesh. Those small fingers danced over his shaft, teasing, tempting, torturing him. Granted, it was mind blowing bliss, but it was also agony.

Then, again, without moving her gaze away from his, she lowered her mouth. With one lick across the crown of his penis, he almost came right there and then. But that was just the proverbial shot across the bow.

She opened her mouth and took him inside. God, her mouth was hot and wet. Her tongue should be registered as a lethal weapon. It slid over his rigid cock, wrapping around him as if he were her favorite treat. With every twist around his cock, she drove him further to the edge, and closer to losing his freaking mind. Fuck, he was so close, he almost came, but he didn't want that. Pulling her up, he turned the tables on her. He rolled them over on the bed, and grabbed her by the hips, pulling her up to his mouth.

She was laughing, then moaned loudly, as he slid his tongue into her sex. She was hot, wet, and tasted just like before. Delicious. He pushed her fast and hard, right up to the edge, then he pulled himself back. When he moved away from her, she growled and he laughed. After grabbing a condom and rolling it on, he took her in hand again and thrust into her. Damn.

It was like coming home.

He held himself still for a long moment, then started to move. He didn't know at that point where one of them stopped and the other started. He was so lost in her that he didn't care. Again, and again, he thrust into her, pushing them both closer to the edge, then pulling back. Then it became imperative to get there, and he wanted to be there with her.

He felt his orgasm approaching, so he reached down between their bodies. He pressed his finger against her clit.

"Come for me, Cat. Come on."

She was moving her head back and forth as if denying him, as if it was too much to take in. But he would not be deterred. He stopped her by leaning down and kissing her. She returned the kiss with an intensity that sent him hurtling over the edge. He couldn't seem to hold himself back anymore. But it did not matter. She bowed up against him and screamed his name. Her orgasm ripped through her, and pulled him deeper into her hot core. Her nails bit into his back as she convulsed against him.

He was there with her, his own release coming in a rush just a second after she had screamed his name. He plunged into her again and gave himself over to pleasure. But he wasn't done. With infinite control, he pulled out and thrust into her one more time, and pushed her over the edge into another orgasm. This one even stronger than the first, from the way her inner muscles tightened on his cock.

He collapsed on top of her, completely wrecked. If he had thought she blew his mind before, this left him deaf, dumb and blind. He felt connected to her on some other level that he had never had with another woman.

"Hey, you're heavy," she said, pushing at him.

He used what little energy he had left to roll off her, then pulled her over with him. He wrapped an arm around her, cupping her rear end. The only word that came to mind was...satisfaction. This woman, in this moment, was all Drew needed.

"I don't know if I can move now," he said.

"We don't have to do anything but go to sleep," she mumbled against his chest.

The comfort of that one statement warmed him from

the inside out. Cat might not think of herself as a comforter, but she was. Even after everything they had been through, he felt safe with her. He drifted off, the feel of her hair against his neck and her hand over this heart.

# CHAPTER FOURTEEN

Drew heard her rustling around looking for clothes at just after six a.m. the next morning. He tried to open his eyes, but it took three times to achieve it. It was still dark in his bedroom. That made sense, since in his mind, it was the middle of the freaking night. It was too early for humans, in his opinion, but he knew Cat got up early.

"Where are you going?" he mumbled.

The sounds of her gathering her things stopped. "Sorry. I didn't mean to wake you."

"No problem," he said as he forced himself to open his eyes. "Just as long as you weren't trying to leave without saying goodbye."

She said nothing for a minute, and he knew that had been her plan. He rolled over to look at her. "Really?"

"I know you don't like to get up early."

She didn't sound convinced of her own argument. He could get mad at her, and in the past, he probably would have. But talking last night had put some of his worries to rest. He knew that they had issues, but much of it stemmed from her upbringing and her sense of worth. He would not allow those to mess with them again.

"And so you were going to sneak out to work?"

"I have to go home."

"Why?"

"Really? I need a shower."

"You could take one here."

"I have no clothes, and I am *not* doing the walk of shame into the office. I also doubt that Del would be happy if I showed up in my board shorts and tank top."

He smiled. "Well, give me a second."

"For what?"

He said nothing as he slipped out of bed to stand beside her. He leaned down and brushed his mouth over hers. "Good morning."

She sighed and leaned closer to deepen the kiss. Just that little gesture had his heart singing. In this, she couldn't hold back. There was no hidden agenda or pretending in this moment. There was only Cat.

He pulled back. "Give me a sec and I'll go with you."

She nodded, but didn't say anything. He had hoped they'd cleared the air last night, but now he was worried she was having second thoughts.

"What's wrong?" she asked.

He shook his head. "Nothing."

"No, there is something. You thought I was trying to run out of here, didn't you?"

"Maybe."

She rolled her eyes and leaned in for another kiss.

"I'm not going to run away anymore. I didn't want to be so brazen about our relationship at work either."

He cocked his head to the side and studied her for a second. "You want to keep it secret?"

"For right now."

So, she didn't want anyone to know they were together now. It irritated him enough that, apparently, she picked up on it.

"Hey. It doesn't have anything to do with the team. It has to do with us. I want to give us some time to just be us. You know with everyone at work, they can be so nosey. We have enough baggage from before that I don't want it to interfere with what is going on now."

"Yeah?"

She nodded. "So, hurry up. I'll make some coffee."

He stood there for a few seconds trying to grasp this new situation. He had never been a man who liked to rush things. Even as a child, he liked to take his time and savor the moment. Last night, though, he had been different. Now, in the light of day, he wanted to spend all day with her; although, he knew that wasn't possible. But he wanted to make that happen, and soon.

First, though, they had a killer to catch. It still didn't mean he couldn't steal a few moments here and there.

With that on his mind, he started the shower, and decided to get ready.

Cat found her way around Drew's kitchen. For a man who grew up in a family that was considered a legend in the restaurant industry, she knew he didn't cook much. She had a secret suspicion that he was a killer cook, but just told people the opposite, so he didn't get roped in to cooking all the time. He seemed to survive on prepackaged food.

She opened the refrigerator door and studied the contents. Good lord, the man needed to go shopping. There was very little perishable food in the refrigerator, but he did have a lot of energy drinks. She shook her head. That couldn't be good for him.

She found his coffee in the freezer. As she filled up the water reservoir for the coffeemaker, she started thinking about how to handle this new relationship. She knew that Drew thought everything was settled, and he had forgiven her. Maybe that was why she hadn't told him before. Drew was one of the most forgiving people she knew, and keeping the truth from him had given her some distance.

Now, she had to deal with this relationship. One she didn't feel she really deserved. Drew was a good man, one that she knew she could count on. And their friendship was something she had cherished since they'd first met. The last year had been so damned hard on her. She hadn't just lost a potential boyfriend, she had lost a very good friend. It wasn't anything new. She was toxic. Drew didn't deserve to be exposed to that, but he apparently didn't care.

Worse, she had hope now. A tiny kernel of optimism had blossomed in her heart, one that she would be smart to kill. She didn't want to. She yearned for this, to have a good man who thought she was special, who treated her with respect. It was something she had wanted for years, but now that it was a possibility, she was sure something would come in and take it away from her. She wasn't sure if she would be able to handle another breakup with Drew like the last one. They had barely started dating, and had never been to bed together. Now that they had been intimate, there was a good chance it would tear a hole in her soul if everything went to shit again.

She closed her eyes as she thought about the night before. When he had kissed her the year before, she had known he would be a good lover. Add in that he was detail oriented, and she knew that he'd know just how to handle her. None of that had prepared her for the night before. She could still feel his hands on her body, see the intense look he gave her when he drove into her each and every time.

Even right now she wanted him. She wanted to have him take her again and damn the consequences. When she found herself contemplating why it wasn't a bad idea to join him in the shower, she pulled herself back from the edge. She opened her eyes and shook her head. Too much work to do. They needed to take this slowly and make sure they didn't hurt each other. She turned on the coffeemaker just as her phone vibrated on the kitchen counter. She saw Del's number and grabbed it immediately.

"Hey, boss. What's up?"

"Nothing really. I got a call on one of the women that

dated all three men, an Amber Tanaka. She was off the island…in fact, out of the country at the time of Anderson's murder. So, she's off the hook."

"Is there a reason that I didn't get that call?"

He sighed. "No. It was the assistant to the chief of police. You know how they work. They think that calling me looks better. All it does is piss me off at six in the morning."

"Sorry."

"No worries. Not your fault. Consequently, that takes us down to two women, and you can tell Drew he doesn't have to set up a date with Ms. Tanaka."

"Sounds good."

There was a pause. "You sound different."

She hesitated. "Uh, okay."

"No, you sound rested. That's good."

She heard a sound behind her and turned to find Drew standing there smiling. His hair was still wet and, good lord, he was shirtless. Little droplets of water glistened on his flesh. The need to walk over to him and lick all of it off almost overwhelmed her. That is, if she weren't talking to her boss on the phone.

"Cat?"

"Sorry," she said as her cheeks grew hot.

She wasn't a prude, and growing up in Hawaii had a lot to do with that. You couldn't spend so much time at the beach and be embarrassed by skin. Being on the phone with her boss while lusting after Drew was an entirely different matter altogether. Especially since the images continued to flash through her brain. God, she wanted to taste every inch of his body.

"I need to finish getting ready and head in. I'll catch Drew up with the new info."

"Good. See ya then."

They hung up and she set her phone down. Drew stood there smiling at her. She could tell from his expression that he was aware of what he was doing to her.

"What?"

He shrugged. "I'm not sure I've ever seen you embarrassed."

"I wasn't embarrassed."

"Liar," he said, as he stepped closer and pulled her against him. "You were. And all because the boss caught us."

"First, he didn't catch us. He just called to say that the Tanaka woman was off the island for the last murder."

"And second?"

"What do you mean?"

"Second? What was the second point that you were making?"

Dammit. One of the things she liked about Drew was his quick mind, but sometimes it was her undoing.

"If you must know, it's because I was on the phone with Del—"

"I knew it."

"You didn't let me finish."

"Sorry." But he didn't look that sorry. In fact, he looked damned smug.

"Fine. It's because I wanted to lick the water off your chest. It normally wouldn't embarrass me, because I am not a prude."

"Thank God for that."

"Still, it was weird having those thoughts while I was on the phone with Del."

He chuckled. "That's actually kind of cute."

"Don't make me punch you in the groin, Franklin."

"Sorry, but it is." He leaned down and brushed his mouth over hers. "I take it that we don't have time for a leisurely breakfast?"

She shook her head. "We need to check out this other woman, and you probably need to set up another date with Lana."

Just saying the woman's name left a bad taste in her mouth.

"Okay. Let me get some travel mugs for the coffee. We could probably hit Rainbow for some breakfast to go."

"Hmm, okay, but we can't eat there."

"Sure thing."

Without warning, he swooped in for a hot, fast, wet kiss that ended as quickly as it had begun. He walked away as if it was an ordinary thing for him to melt her brain with a kiss. The man was going to kill her with lust before this was all over.

Watching from across the street, she saw Drew leave his apartment building with a woman. The woman looked vaguely familiar, but now, she couldn't place her. It didn't matter who she was. What mattered was that she had spent the night. She did not doubt it. A red haze of rage filled her vision as she watched him follow the other woman to her car.

Jealousy and anger twisted in her gut, as she watched Drew stop and kiss the woman before getting into the vehicle. It was sweet, and it left a bad taste in her mouth. This man had pretended to get his way. He had said he was looking for love. A liar, like all the rest. Always lying. He was involved with a woman, *that* woman. The intimacy she witnessed told of a longer relationship. It wasn't just a one night stand. There had been affection, and it had left her shivering in anger.

And for that, she would make him pay.

# TANGLED PASSIONS

# CHAPTER FIFTEEN

Adam tapped his fingers on the table as he waited for Jin to show up. He'd taken Elle's advice and called Jin. Truthfully, he was amazed she had taken his phone call. Since he'd gotten her into rehab, he'd had minimal contact with her. She had said she needed the time to heal, and he had let her have it. So, when she suggested Wailana Coffee House for breakfast this morning, he wasn't going to argue. Sadly, he'd shown up ten minutes early.

He saw her outside the window on the street. She looked, good. Clearly better than she had the last time he had seen her. And Elle was right. She had gained wait and it looked good on her.

She stepped into the diner and spotted him immediately. A rush of excitement filtered through him as he watched her walk to the booth where he was sitting. He couldn't help it. Even though it had been years since they'd had a romantic relationship, the feelings he'd had for her were still there.

Her face had filled out, and she now had her hair cut short again. Yes, she was *definitely* looking good. Adam remembered his manners and slipped out of the booth to wait for her to be seated.

"Adam," she said, smiling at him. Then she slid into the booth opposite of his seat. He followed suit.

She opened her mouth to say something, but the waitress had hurried over. "I would love a cup of coffee, with cream."

The waitress left them alone.

Jin grinned at him. "You look good, Adam."

"As do you."

"Thank you. I'm glad you called. I wasn't sure if you would be interested in talking to me again."

"Why would you feel that way?"

She sighed and her smile slipped away. "You kept having to bail me out of jail."

He shook his head. After her assault, Jin had a rough time coping. Hell, anyone would. First, she'd refused to leave the house, then she became the life of the party. Her drinking had landed her at HPD a few times before he could convince her to go into rehab.

"You're my friend, Jin. I wouldn't turn my back on you."

She smiled as the waitress put the cup of coffee in front of her.

"Would you like to order?"

Jin nodded and ordered pancakes, which Adam did as well. When they were finally alone, she doctored her coffee.

"It's good you have your appetite back."

"Thanks to rehab, yes. Lots of counseling. I have to thank you for that. I lost so many friends over the last couple of years. Even before I became a belligerent drunk."

"I would have to say they weren't friends then."

She took a sip of coffee, then set her cup down. "I think you're right. I've been thinking about calling you, but I didn't know how you would take it. Elle encouraged me to, and I know it's one of the steps."

"To make amends."

She nodded. "I do owe you an apology. For before my abduction and after."

He hated that she felt like that. "You have nothing to apologize for."

"No, I do. You know when I first saw you, what I

thought?"

He shook his head.

"I thought, now how is this fine man walking toward me? All the women watched you walk across the lawn. Even better, you made a beeline for me."

He felt his face heating and she laughed, a true genuine laugh. It was corny to say, but it was music to his ears. He hadn't heard it for well over a year. Before the attack, she had always been so happy.

"Oh, my. Seeing you blush just made my day. But it's true. And then, I used you."

"Now—"

"No, I did. You and I both know it. I used you as a source for my reporting, and I always regretted it. For that I want to apologize. And I want to thank you."

"For what?"

"You kept contact with me when everyone else left. After I was no longer a storyline, my old friends dumped me, left me without any lifelines. Elle was there...thank God for her. That woman deserves a medal for the work she does. But there was also you."

"You don't drop friends because they go through a rough patch."

She studied him for a long moment. "Some people do. You didn't. And every time I wanted to end it all, to make the pain go away, you'd show up."

The idea that she wanted to commit suicide left him cold. She was a vibrant woman, with so much to offer. The thought that she would have taken her own life was sickening.

"I owe you so much."

"I don't want that."

She blinked. "What?"

"I just want to be friends. If I go through a bad time, then be there. You don't owe me anything."

She studied him, searching his gaze with her own, then she nodded. "You got it. I can't promise I won't be a total idiot again, or that every day with me will be easy. There are still days I want to crawl into a dark space and stay there for a thousand years."

"But you don't."

"Sometimes, I do go to the dark place. I don't want to hurt myself anymore, but there are moments when I need a break. I need the quiet."

"As long as you come back out of it when you're ready, that's all that matters. One day at a time."

"Yes, as goofy as that sounds. Taking it one day at a time helps. It makes my life manageable."

"So, tell me what you're working on," he said.

She gave him the thousand-watt smile that he remembered. "I've decided to freelance, and I'm going to start a blog about the islands."

He sat back and listened to her talk about her plans for the next few months, contented that she seemed so sure of her life.

Drew enjoyed the drive over to Cat's house. He liked the windward side of the island, and had lived there until moving into the condo. Well, first he'd stayed with Charity in her guest room, then he moved into the condo. It had been easier for work, but he had missed the different feel of this side of the island. He loved the rolling hills, all the green trees, and the waterfalls that came to life in a heavy rain.

He particularly liked taking the Pali with Cat driving. It was kind of dorky, but he loved that he was spending this time with her. It was away from work, just the two of them with FM100 on the radio, and the sweet morning air blowing through her SUV. She'd pulled her hair back so it wasn't blowing in her face, but the wind would occasionally pick up strands.

"You're not mad I want to keep our relationship a secret, are you?" she asked.

He glanced at her, then smiled. "No worries. I like the idea of keeping it from the work *ohana*. They can be a bit too nosey like you said."

She snorted as she took the exit to her neighborhood. "That is sort of calling the kettle black."

"Both of us are guilty, but I think you're right. We need to keep this just between us. It would put too much pressure on us. Plus, if everyone knows, it could really cause problems with the case."

Damn, he talked a good game. He wanted everyone to know they were together now. It was going to take the entirety of his self-control not to blurt it out to Charity, but he would do as she asked. It had been a little unnerving when everyone was watching them last time. They could take their time and not have to worry about what anyone else was thinking.

She pulled into her driveway and he smiled. He loved this little house. He knew people would think he was crazy, but this was the real Hawaii to him. It was nice to have the view he had at the more modern condo apartment, but this spoke to his soul. It always did. He didn't need a massive house, although, he knew he could afford one. He liked this house sitting on a corner lot with neighbors who had probably been there for decades. This is what made Hawaii real to him.

The house was over eighty years old, built in what they called a plantation style of house. She had painted it the traditional green last year. There were two plumeria trees out front, which only added to the charm. She now had flower beds and a few shrubs too, including a rather large hibiscus bush.

Then, he noticed the other changes.

"Hey, I like those shutters."

She glanced at him, then slid out of the SUV. "I did that a few months ago. I thought it would look nice."

"It does."

He followed her up the walkway to the front steps. Someone shouted her name, and Cat said something under her breath. He turned and saw a smiling woman wearing a moo moo standing in the yard across the street. Her mostly gray hair was down to her waist, but she had it pulled back into a ponytail. She was holding a coffee cup in one hand and waving with the other.

"Hey, Auntie Koko," she said. "Howzit?"

"Doing great."

She looked like she wanted to be introduced to Drew, but Cat had other plans.

"I have to get to work, so I'll chat with you later."

The woman wasn't offended, from the smiles she kept giving them. Drew glanced back at the older woman a couple of times as she stood on the corner smiling at them.

Cat unlocked the door and stepped into her house. Drew followed her in.

"Sorry about that. I just hope she doesn't call my mother."

"No problem. You know I know how to handle aunties."

She smiled at him. "I think most Hawaiians are born with the ability, or you learn it before grade school at least."

They stared at each other and something changed. A charge lit the air and right then and there, he wanted her again. He took two steps to reach her. She came willingly into his arms. Without hesitation, he crushed his mouth down on hers. It was insane that he wanted her this much, it almost consumed him. He slipped his tongue between her lips, allowing it to glide against hers. He needed to be closer to her, so he skimmed his hands down to cup her ass to draw her against him. When he did, he felt the hard points of her nipples through their layers of clothing.

He wanted her. Then, and without thinking of the

consequences. He wanted nothing more than to strip her clothes off and bury himself inside of her.

That thought had him pulling back. When he did, they both stared at each other, breathing heavily.

"Well," she said as she gulped in huge amounts of air. "That escalated quickly."

Even though he was painfully aroused, he chuckled. "Yeah, it did. But we need to get to work. I would much rather stay here, but I want this case over as soon as possible."

"Yeah."

Yet, she didn't move. She stood there and stared at him. Drew curled his fingers into the palms of his hands.

"Go before I change my mind."

She gave him a smile that had so much power in it, he felt it down to the soles of his feet. The woman really had no idea how amazing she looked. He knew she didn't because she would surely let it go to her head. Cat seemed unaware of what she did to him. That confident grin had his fingers itching to touch her body again.

"Okay."

Still, she took her time, walking slowly down the hall. He watched the sway of her hips, then she paused and he raised his gaze to hers. For a long moment, he felt it there, the connection he had never felt with anyone else. It was like that one and only date they had had. The memory of that one kiss still left him half aroused. He had never been what anyone would consider a player when it came to women, but he'd dated, and he wasn't a virgin. But that kiss...it had been a life changing moment for him. Cat had felt it, he was sure.

He stood there for a second trying to calm his arousal down, and wondered just what that last look meant. He knew it had been one night, but he also knew it was the same feeling as before...only stronger. The expression on her face told him as much, but it said something else. She knew her power, or was just gaining it. She was confident in every aspect of her professional life, but Drew knew she didn't see herself as exceptionally pretty.

He heard her turn on the water in the shower, and almost gave in. It would be so easy to make his way to the bathroom and take a shower with her. Water, soap, and Cat. That would make for an interesting morning following their most amazing night. With a sigh, he tore his mind away from that image. They had to get to work, and he needed to keep his head on straight.

To distract himself, he looked around her house. Drew had been to Cat's house before. She'd had a few parties, but he hadn't been able to look around much. Mainly because it would have looked creepy skulking around like that. But now that she was in the shower, he took the time to investigate, to familiarize himself with her a little more.

There was a small but orderly kitchen with a dining area. She had Hawaiian accents there, from the towels to the oven mitts. The kitchen spilled out into a living area where she had a big couch that he knew was beyond comfortable. She had shelves and more shelves in there. Some held books, which consisted of mainly manuals about crime scene investigation. There were pictures everywhere. It was easy to see how much she loved her family. All girls without a father, and Cat was the one who held them together. The girls all seemed to love Cat; although, he knew it was a hard role to take. She wasn't the oldest, but they always looked to her to fix things.

Then, he saw a picture of Cat and her mother. It had to be the day Cat graduated from the Academy. Cat was smiling into the camera, but the look on her mother's face only spoke of worry. He was certainly acquainted with that feeling. He wasn't lying the night before. Every time she went out, he worried. But then, there were other pictures. They were standing at the top of Diamond Head, mother and daughter with their arms around each other, and they were laughing into the camera. She might complain about her mother, but there was no doubt after seeing that picture. They loved each other.

Another thing that made him love her even more. She might not believe him right now, but he did love her. He'd been infatuated with her since the moment they'd met.

It hadn't been just her looks, but it was the whole aura of the woman. Tough, smart, but as time went by, he had found that hard exterior as fascinating as the soft side she tried to hide from him and everyone else in the world. It made him feel special in a way. And that is why he loved her. It was probably what made him so angry over the last year. He hated himself for loving her.

As he debated if he should make coffee or not, there was a knock at the door. Seems Auntie Koko didn't want to wait until later, he thought with a smile. He was still grinning as he opened the door and found Cat's mother standing on the stoop.

His smile faded as his brain stopped working for a moment or two. Mrs. Kalakau stood there, a frown on her face, and her eyes sparking with wrath.

Oh, this was bad. Cat's mother was half Hawaiian and half Korean. She leaned toward the side of Korean when it came to her daughters. Very traditional, and a bit of an authoritarian.

"Mrs. Kalakau." Damn, his voice almost cracked.

"Andrew." She nodded. "I hear you just brought my daughter home, and I want to know what is going on."

# TANGLED PASSIONS

# CHAPTER SIXTEEN

Cat was tugging her shirt on when she heard her mother's voice. That couldn't be right. Her mother never just popped over to see her. *Ever.* Then, she remembered Auntie Koko yelling over at her. She was one of her mother's spies.

And, if her mother was there, Drew was having to deal with her. Dammit. For a very long moment, she thought about waiting it out. It didn't make her proud that she seriously thought about leaving Drew to cope with her mother.

She looked at herself in the mirror and sighed. She didn't want to lose Drew over this. Not many men could deal with her mother. With much trepidation, she opened the door to her bathroom.

"Cat did not tell me that you were helping her with the case."

"Oh?" she heard Drew say. "She probably isn't allowed to do that. It's kind of hush hush, you know. Do you take sugar in your coffee?"

"No. Sugar makes you fat."

"I like a woman who knows what she wants."

There was a long silence. At that point, she decided to

quit being a coward and save Drew. She walked down the hallway, dread weighing heavily on her shoulders. She was not prepared for what she saw. Drew was sitting at her small dining table with her mother, talking about his mother and father, as if they were at a Sunday social at church.

"Catherine," her mother said.

"Mom. What are you doing here so early?"

"I got a call from Koko."

"Of course you did. I'm going to write her up for those expired tags on her car."

Her mother frowned. "You will not."

Her mother never did understand Cat's dry sense of humor. Her sister said it was generational, but it wasn't that. Her mother took everything literally. All humor flew over her head.

"What are you doing here, besides her calling you?"

"I was worried. I did not know who this man was that Koko saw with you."

More than likely, her mother thought she would catch her doing something illicit; and, of course, she would have if Drew hadn't turned her down.

"I was just talking about the case, but I didn't tell her much."

"You have your first lead," her mother said, an accusatory tone in her voice.

"I told you that."

"Well, I did not know that you had dragged Drew into it."

"She didn't drag me. Besides, I was happy to help. This person is killing other people. Cat's going to catch her."

"Her?" her mother asked.

"Yes, we think it is a woman. Cat is convinced of it."

Then, Cat watched as her mother turned and smiled at Drew. It was a genuine one too. The one she reserved for Father Alan at church. He met Cat's eyes over the top of his coffee cup. There was a smug humor there that almost made her want to punch him as much as she wanted to laugh.

"Do quit hovering, Catherine," her mother ordered. "It isn't very ladylike."

She wanted to tell her mother to shove it, but that would end with a fight. She didn't have time to make nice with her mother. If she explained it, her mother would just come up with some other reason why she needed to talk to Cat. Thankfully, Drew must have sensed her irritation and her thought process, and he stepped in.

"We really have to go. Cat has to give an update on the case to the crew."

Her mother looked at her and then back to Drew. "Okay."

Cat blinked. Who was this creature? The one that seemed to be okay with doing anything Drew told her to? She walked her mother to the door and out onto the stoop.

"I thought maybe you had a man here."

"If I did, it wouldn't be any of your business."

"You are always my business."

She sighed. "What I mean is that I am an adult. And while I appreciate you wanting to watch over me, I can take care of myself."

Her mother walked out to the car and Cat followed. She knew that wasn't the end of the conversation.

"You know, I always worried about you."

"Yes, Mama."

"But, you were always strong. Even after we lost your father, you were the one there, taking care of the others, cooking dinner, and keeping the house clean."

She said nothing, as she watched her mother get into the car. Then, her mother sat there, saying nothing for a long time.

"You don't have to be the person who does everything."

"What does that mean?"

"It means that every now and then, it is good to let someone else carry the load for you. You don't always have to be the strong one."

It was the closest thing to a real conversation they had had in months. She had missed this part of the relationship, where they had real conversations and did things together. Of course, her mother being who she was, had to ruin it.

"Call your sister."

Then she started the car and backed it up. Cat stood there completely confused by what just happened. She watched her mother drive all the way down the street until she could no longer see her taillights. Then, she turned to walk back in the house. Drew was standing there, leaning against the doorjamb, a coffee mug in his hand.

"Everything okay?"

She nodded as she walked up to him. "I think she likes you more than she likes me."

"That is understandable."

"Let's get going. I have a meeting to put together, and you have another date to make with our suspect."

"If you say so, boss."

She shook her head and reminded herself not to let her emotions take over. There was no telling where they were headed after this, but she knew that for right now, everything was fine. She was just probably feeling weird because her mother had thrown her for a loop.

Cat was reading over a report of Lana's financials, noting there was something off about them. They looked almost a little too perfect. She was just about to pull up another document when there was a knock on the doorjamb. She turned around and found Autumn standing there. Great.

"Hey, there."

"Did you need something?" she asked, trying to be professional and probably failing. She had a problem with hiding her true feelings. Always had.

Autumn didn't take the hint. Instead, she stepped into Cat's office and shut the door.

"I feel like we got off on the wrong foot, and I wanted to set things straight."

"Okay. But I don't think there is anything wrong."

Autumn chuckled them. "Oh, please. You gave me a death glare when I was talking to Drew. I didn't know you two were an item."

"We aren't. Or we weren't." Dammit. One day and she was spilling secrets to the new girl. "We...never mind."

"That sounds all interesting. Care to share?" Autumn said, sitting in the chair. Again, she did this uninvited. Cat had a feeling that she and Autumn were not going to get along.

"No. Not really."

Autumn deflated a bit. "Okay. Just know that I didn't know I was poaching on goods. I don't do that. Sharing is not something I'm good at."

"Didn't you grow up in a commune?"

"No, I grew up in a cult, and you had to share *everything*. Absolutely everything. It was insane. Food, water, clothes, pencils, the works. I drew the line at underwear, because that's just gross."

"I have to agree with you on that."

"So, I'm kind of possessive of things, including my men. But I wanted you to know that I would never do that to another woman. Not my thing."

She couldn't help it. Cat smiled. "Thanks. Although, nothing really happened."

"Please. I could smell the hormones in the air this morning."

Cat frowned. "During the meeting?"

Autumn nodded. "I almost got a contact high from it."

"Damn."

"Don't worry. I don't think anyone else noticed. I mean, they know you two are hot for each other, and there is some kind of office poll going on, but I don't think they picked up on it."

"But you did?"

She nodded. "Well, you know, when you grow up with a bunch of people around you all the time, you know the signs."

"How long did you live in the cult?" Realizing how rude that was, especially since she coveted her privacy, she immediately regretted the question. Sorry, that was kind of nosey."

"Not at all. I have never hidden my strange beginnings. I assumed everyone here knew, but I was there until I was sixteen."

"Did your parents leave with you?"

She chuckled. "No. My father was the leader."

Cat blinked. "Your father was the leader? As in the..."

"The David Koresh of Hawaii? Yeah. My father was in the bonkers category. I always wondered what it would be like with a normal father, but then I think I might have turned out kind of boring."

"I have so many questions."

"Emma did as well. That girl's mind never stops working. But," she said looking over her shoulder, "I think you have company."

There, in the window, she could see Drew loitering.

"He really is cute. I hope you know how lucky you are."

"I'm starting to understand," she said.

"Hey," Autumn said as she passed Drew. "She's all yours."

"What was that about?"

Cat shrugged and kept looking at him. "What do you want?"

"That is definitely a loaded question."

She smiled. "Yeah?"

"Yeah. I was wondering," he said, closing the door. "If you wanted to come over tonight. We could grill something, hang out."

She sighed. It sounded like heaven to her, but she had to keep her head screwed on straight. "I don't think that's a good idea."

"Why not?"

"What if this Lana chick is the woman who is after you? What do you think she would say if she saw me coming out of your building in the morning?"

He sighed. "Still, who cares? That would probably just speed up the process. Maybe she would go crazy then and attack me."

The idea of him getting hurt again sent a cold chill sliding down her spine. "Don't joke around about that."

He picked up on her tone. "I'm sorry. So, tonight?"

"No. I don't think it is a good idea."

He cocked his head to the side and studied her. "Is there another reason?"

"No." Not really.

"Catherine."

"Don't use that name. My mother and Father Alan are the only two people who can call me by that name."

He smiled. "Quit avoiding the subject."

"I don't want to go too fast."

Drew stared at her for a long moment, then he started to laugh.

"What?"

He shook his head. "I'm sorry, but I don't think anyone would think that we moved too fast. I've been working on you for about four years."

It was her turn to stare. "What are you talking about?"

"You have to know I was infatuated with you from the first moment I met you."

She could play coy, but Cat didn't play well at that game. "I knew you might be attracted."

He snorted. "And don't tell me that you weren't

intrigued."

The man was getting a little too cocky. "Nah, I barely remembered your name."

Instead of getting mad, he chuckled.

"So, tell me why you can't come over?"

She hesitated because she had no real reason. "I need some clothes. It is hard enough to make it in here in the morning on time."

"Good, then it's settled."

"Wait, what?"

"I'll come over to your place. We'll stop by my place, pick up some clothes, then grab dinner on the way home."

He said it like it was completely normal. Home. As if he lived with her. He hadn't even spent the night there, and he was assuming they would spend the night together. She should object. She had always liked having her own space and being on her own. But, there was this tiny part of her rejoicing at the idea. She rarely felt comfortable with men, but with Drew, she always felt centered. And they would be able to work on the strategy for his next date.

"Did you call Lana?" she asked.

The gleam in his eyes told her he knew she was trying to divert the conversation, but apparently, he was going to let her off the hook for now.

"Yes. Tomorrow night."

"Good."

A few beats of silence went by before he said, "So, your place or mine?"

She knew she should say no. Rushing things could end up badly for them both, but he was smiling at her, and being with him made Cat feel good. It was insane that a man who was so different than she was seemed to know exactly what she needed.

"Fine. We'll stay at your place, but I need to get a few things."

"I don't mind staying at your place."

"I know that, but do you want to deal with Auntie

Koko again?"

"Good point."

He closed the blinds, then walked over to her. "What are you doing?"

He said nothing as he pulled her up out of her chair and into his arms. "How about I pick something up while you head back to your place and get your stuff?"

"Are you trying to manage me, Franklin?"

He kissed her nose. "Just a little."

"I'm not sure I like that."

"You do. You just have to get used to it."

She opened her mouth to argue with him, but he kissed her. Quick, hard, and mind meltingly good. When he pulled back, he was smiling.

"My place then? And how about some grilled shrimp?"

Dammit, he was just too cute to say no to.

"Shrimp sounds good."

"Great. I'll head out now and get the stuff I need." He gave her another kiss, this one more leisurely, but just as powerful. "I better go now before we get found out."

He stepped back and opened the office door. When he stepped out, he laughed. She followed him out. There, in the conference room, was most of the team.

"Is there a meeting I didn't know about?" she asked.

"Nope," Charity said with a smile.

She looked at Drew. "Del said to delegate, so this is your mess."

"Coward," he muttered.

"You bet," she said as she walked back to her office and shut the door.

Drew stood there, abandoned by Cat, and knew he was going to have to answer questions. Closing her blinds probably wasn't the smartest thing to have done. All the agents had their own offices, which had a massive window out into the conference area. There were only a few times any of them closed their blinds, and one of them would be for privacy.

"So," Emma said. "You got anything to say?"

"Nope. Other than I have a date tomorrow night."

Emma shared a look with Charity. "Where are you taking her?"

"I thought maybe a movie. We're meeting over at the Ward Cinema."

"I have a feeling he's talking about the suspect," Marcus said.

"You thought I was talking about someone else?" Drew asked, trying to sound innocently confused on the subject.

Elle frowned. "Drew Franklin, don't tell me I dragged my very swollen feet up here only to find out you were talking about work?"

"Hey, I didn't say that you should come up here. I was just meeting with Cat about the date tomorrow night."

They all stared at him and he almost broke. It was hard not to want to shout it out loud, because he wanted everyone to know. He had serious doubts from looking at all of their coworkers, that they would be able to keep it a secret for long.

"Fine," Emma said. "You heard him. We have to wait for confirmation for the bet."

"What bet?" Del said from his office doorway.

"Uh," Emma said, then she directed a thousand-watt smile in her husband's direction. "Nothing."

With the boss giving everyone the death glare, the crowd dispersed. Everyone left except for Charity.

"Hey, are you sure you're okay?" she asked.

"I'm fine. Don't worry about me."

"I do though. I worry about you both. I won't allow you to be hurt again. Either one of you."

He took her hand and gave it a light squeeze.

"Sometimes, risking hurt is more important than keeping your heart safe."

She rolled her eyes. "Good lord, you sound like a Hallmark Channel movie."

"You like those, so you can't complain. You made me watch all those damned Christmas movies last year. I still have nightmares."

She smiled, but didn't laugh like he hoped she would.

"I just want you to be okay."

"I'm okay. Don't worry, mama."

"But I will. Please don't go to the dark place."

He frowned. "What are you talking about?"

"After the shooting, you were kind of an asshole."

"I was not. And besides, even if I was, I had been shot. I think that warrants being an asshole."

She shook her head. "Make sure to remember, you always have friends."

"Thanks, Charity. As a reminder, if something goes wrong, maybe we're both at fault."

She nodded, then kissed his cheek and walked toward the elevators. He watched her until she disappeared around the corner, all the while thinking about what she had said. Then, as if unable to resist, he glanced toward Cat's window. The blinds were still shut. They had things to work out, but right now, there was no rush.

Instead of worrying about that, he headed out the door. He had some food to pick up and a dinner to plan.

# TANGLED PASSIONS

# CHAPTER SEVENTEEN

Drew pulled the shrimp and asparagus off the grilling pan, and smiled over at Cat. When she had shown up thirty minutes earlier, he had been delighted by the way she had dressed. Cat wasn't a woman who went for glamour all the time, but she'd worn a bright red sundress with thin straps. It was one of the few times she had pulled her hair up into a messy bun on top of her head. It wasn't that he needed these little gestures, because he found her equally stunning when she strapped on her gear to go out to work, but it was a nice change of pace.

She stood close to the open window, drinking a glass of wine, and looking out over the water. A light wind played with the few stands of hair that had escaped her bun.

"Hey, dinner's ready."

She turned and smiled at him. Just that small gesture left him speechless. All this time, and nothing had changed. He'd been mad at her for the last few months, but deep down, he had also been mad at himself. No matter how irritated he'd been with her, he still wanted her. She would piss him off, and they wouldn't be speaking, but she would smile and he would forget all about it.

"It smells amazing."

He couldn't think of what he should say next. He stood there staring at her. The picture she presented was amazing. The sun was beginning to set behind her, the last red orange rays sparked over the sky and glittered off the glass in the room.

"Are you all right?"

Shaking his head, he said, "Not really, but it isn't a big thing."

Except that it was. He was fucking in love with her. Sure, he had that fuzzy idea of really being infatuated with her, but never in his mind had he thought about those feelings past that initial phase. He had used that word love in his own head this morning. It was just now that he realized she was the most important person in his life. How the hell had that happened? How did he deal with the fact that she worked a dangerous job, and he could lose her on one bad day? When the hell had this happened to him, and how did he not think of the consequences?

"Really, Drew, you're starting to scare me."

He blinked and brought himself back from the edge of fear. "Sorry. Come on, let's eat."

He set the plate of food on the little table that he'd brought to the small area in front of the windows.

"Do you need any more wine?" he asked. She shook her head. "I'll go get the rice and we can eat."

She sat down at the table, and he watched her a second or two before heading back into the kitchen for the rice. When he returned, she was watching the boats out on the water.

"I love this view. I wish I could afford something closer to the water."

"Really?" he asked, sitting down in the opposite chair. "I like your house."

She made a face. "It was all I could afford for rent. Auntie Koko made me a good deal though. Normally, I would be lucky to afford a one-room apartment."

He knew that she was good with her money, but she helped her mother with bills. That would eat away at an officer's paycheck.

"I like that it's real Hawaii. Old plantation house, and you have a lot of land around you. If you owned the house, you could easily expand."

"Ugh, it's been hard enough doing the minor updates I'm doing there right now."

"But you don't own it. Shouldn't that be Auntie Koko's job?"

Cat shrugged as she spooned some rice, then the shrimp and asparagus onto her plate. "She's elderly, and she's on her own. Plus, she gave me a good deal on the house, like I said."

And that was most important to her. Cat had always been the one that helped, the one who took care of the hard stuff. But at the end of the day, who helped Cat? She always seemed to be running on empty, handling a job and an interfering mother. Her sisters weren't much better, always wanting her to protect them from their mother's wrath. Still, he couldn't say anything. Cat was fiercely loyal to her family, and he couldn't really complain about that. It was one of the things he loved about her.

"Still, I like your house better."

She looked out over the water again, then back at him. "You're crazy."

He chuckled. "Undoubtedly, but that won't change my mind. There is a sense of community on your street. You might find it annoying, but you know that if there was something wrong, your neighbors would notice. Not sure I've seen more than one or two residents here."

"Well, there was a reason Emma liked this apartment."

"Yeah, but for me, it's hard. I like the view and I like that I can walk to work, but when I really find a place of my own, it'll be like yours. Real Hawaii. It reminds me of my parents' street. You know your neighbors."

She shook her head as she forked a bite of the rice and shrimp into her mouth. Then she moaned. "Lord Jesus, this is delicious. Why do you work in a morgue cutting people up when you can cook like this?"

He shrugged. "I was in the kitchen by the time I was five, and worked all of my teenage years in one or another of our restaurants. I love to cook, but if I had to do it for paying customers, I might have to kill someone once a week. My family agrees."

"I doubt that."

"No. I have an issue with people who want perfection, or who think they know what tastes better. Add in the fact that my parents think that the customer is always right. I do not."

She laughed and took a sip of wine. "I have to agree with that."

He watched her then, the smile and the sound of her laughter made him regret the next subject they had to cover.

With a sigh of regret, he said, "So, about that date tomorrow."

Her smile faded, and he almost regretted bringing it up. "Yeah?"

"Do you think it's a good idea to have you listening in?"

"What?"

He had to come up with the right way to say it, but it was difficult. He didn't want to step on her toes. "I mean, we're involved now. I thought it might be weird for you."

She blinked, her expression unreadable. "It's my job."

"Yeah, but—"

"No. If I can't handle you on a fake date, I have no business running this investigation."

He wanted to argue, but he knew that tone. She did not suffer fools. Plus, in the end, he would end up losing the argument. So why borrow trouble?

"Did you talk to your mom again today?" he asked

She shook her head. "I got a couple texts from her, and one voicemail from my sister warning me that my mom was on her way to the house. Of course, I didn't see it early enough."

"What difference does it make that she would know about us?"

"First of all, it isn't just you. Any man at my house in the morning better have a damned good reason for being there. Secondly, she would get the idea that we were in a serious relationship."

"And? Is there something wrong with that?"

"Drew."

"No, I want to have an answer to my question. It isn't that I'm proposing anything other than dating." At least right now, he thought. But he could see it clearly. A beach wedding at sunset, both their families there and their work *ohana*…it would rock.

"Earth to Drew?"

He blinked. "Sorry. So, what were we talking about? Oh, yeah, about having a serious relationship. Would that be a bad thing?"

"You don't understand."

He took her hand, and brushed his mouth over her knuckles. "Explain it to me then."

"I told you. I'm not good at relationships."

"Yeah. But I don't think that means much right now. Why are you bad at relationships?"

"I'm self-centered and a workaholic."

He would agree with the second one, but not the first. She was anything but self-centered in his opinion. She just thought she wasn't worthy, and he didn't understand what that really meant until this moment.

"You aren't self-centered."

"But I am a workaholic."

He shrugged. "Doesn't mean you can't have good relationships."

"Stop."

"Stop what?"

"Wishing things were different isn't going to change anything. It will just hurt even more when it falls apart."

"What makes you think it will all fall apart?"

She sighed and looked out the window. "It did last time."

She wanted a chance at happiness. He could hear it in her voice. She just had to believe in it or it would never happen.

"That's because you fucked it up. You won't this time."

Her mouth opened, then snapped shut.

"Nothing to say to that?"

She tried to wrestle her hand away from him, but he refused to let go.

"Drew."

"Cat." He gave her hand one last kiss, then released it. "I won't let you screw us up this time, but I promise, I'm not going to be pushy, okay?"

She crossed her arms beneath her breasts and glared at him. Drew smiled. With her hair up like that, and wearing the little sundress, she looked like a very angry fairy. A lethal fairy, but still a fairy.

"Eat your food. It's going to get cold."

"You're not going to listen to me, are you?"

He shrugged. "I guess I could, but what's going to happen is going to happen."

He started eating again and acting like nothing had happened. She was silent for a moment or two, then she sighed and started eating.

"So, this date tomorrow?" she asked.

"Yeah, I thought maybe a movie? I suggested we meet at Ward and maybe have dinner. But in a theater, it would be easy to have someone in there."

She blinked. "That's a good idea. Movies can be tricky, since it is dark, but she doesn't know our people, which would make it easy to have someone sitting right behind you."

"Good. Not you."

"No. I can handle listening, but I don't want to be there for the whole thing."

He smiled as he forked a bite of asparagus into his

mouth. It wasn't an admission of undying love, but he would take it for now.

In the darkened picnic area below, a woman watched and waited. She could not see much without her binoculars, and she had to be careful that no one saw her. She was even taking a risk here, watching, but she had avoided the traffic cams, as usual.

With a glance to make sure no one was watching, she raised the binoculars to see what was happening. She knew he was a liar, knew that he was going to be her next. And soon. With pain in her heart, she watched as he took the other woman by the hand and lead her back into the apartment. There was no doubt what he had planned along with the romantic dinner, the intimate conversation…rage burned hot in her belly. Her throat ached from the need to scream, but she could not do it here. She needed some place private to vent her anger.

Then, she would be safe to plot his death.

# TANGLED PASSIONS

# CHAPTER EIGHTEEN

The next morning, Cat snuggled deeper in bed. She truly didn't want to wake up, which was odd for her. She had always been known as an early riser, and she loved that. In a house full of women, she had enjoyed the quiet morning times she could have all to herself. She also took pride in the fact that she could work on very little sleep. Today, though, she needed a little extra sleep. Since the start of the case, though, she had been getting very little rest. First, she had been so damned swamped playing catch up on the murders. Then, there was Drew.

The man was wearing her out emotionally and physically. She knew he was one of those still waters kinds of guys. He seemed easygoing on the surface, but there was a lot going on beneath the surface. She knew something had been bothering him last night, but he held back from sharing with her. If she laid there and thought about it, she would never get back to sleep.

She pushed her worries out of her mind and rolled over. Bright light hit her face and she frowned. Before she could contemplate why the blinds weren't drawn, she felt a hand skim up her leg, then between both legs, easing them apart.

A rush of heat rolled through her as Drew's tongue

took the same path, sliding over her sensitive inner thighs. He didn't rush. Instead, he meandered, taking his time as he teased and tasted her. She lifted her head and looked down at him. He finally made his way to her sex, and he caught her gaze with his own. As he leaned down to give her slit one long lick, he kept eye contact. It was like their first night together. He wasn't overtly controlling her, but at this moment, she could not look away. The way he held her gaze, it was as if he were daring her to look away. He knew her so well.

He gave her one last lick before dipping his tongue inside of her sex. It was only then that she let her eyes close. Again and again, he slid between her pussy lips as he built her need. At first, he seemed to be taking it easy, slowly, but soon, it apparently wasn't enough. He slipped his hands beneath her rear end and lifted her off the bed as he rose to his knees. Then, he feasted on her. Over and over, he dove into her core, only stopping to pull her clit between his teeth with a gentle tug, then back again to inside of her. He repeated the gesture, taking her to the very edge, but not enough to push her over. Frustration had her growling because he had complete control. With her legs over his shoulders and her ass off the mattress, she had no way of changing anything. She was left to the mercy of his ministrations.

Delicious heat spiraled through her entire body, dancing over her nerve endings. When he took her clit into his mouth and sucked, Cat hurtled over into pleasure. She convulsed and screamed his name so loudly, she was damned sure the entire building had heard her. As she continued to shake, he slipped his tongue inside her again as her orgasm seemed to go on and on.

Moments later, shivers still racked her body when he laid her back down on the mattress. But he obviously wasn't done with her. He grabbed a condom and rolled it on. He lifted her by the hips, and without hesitation, he entered her, hard and deep, almost pushing her into another orgasm. She was still sensitive from her last release, but that only added another level of painful ecstasy.

Like before, he took his time, thrusting into her long and slow, building her back up. When he leaned down to kiss her, she tasted herself on his lips, on his tongue. She sucked on his tongue, pulling a groan from him, but still, he moved with measured thrusts. He was doing it on purpose, trying to control the situation. At times it was exhilarating, but at the moment, it was driving her insane.

With determination, she wrapped her arms around his neck as she deepened the kiss. Then she planted her feet on the bed and attempted to control the rhythm. He allowed it for a second or two, but then, he tore his mouth away.

"You are very naughty, Cat."

Before she knew what he was doing, he pulled back, flipped her over onto her stomach. With fast, and controlled moves, he pulled her up to her knees and entered her from behind. He had effectively taken control of the situation again. She wanted to fight it, to win the battle of control, then he started to move within her. Harder, faster, deeper. Hunger built her need beyond anything she had ever experienced before. The sound of flesh on flesh filled the room and, just when she was ready to scream in frustration, her orgasm slammed into her.

This time it had shaken her to her core.

"Again," Drew said, just as the last of her release was fading away. He did not stop, not until he made her come twice more, each one more intense than the last one.

As she lost herself in her last orgasm, he groaned her name. His fingers dug into her hips as he plunged into her once more and came. He held himself still as he gave himself over to the pleasure they had created.

He collapsed a moment later, his heart beating hard against her back. He rolled over, taking her with him. She snuggled against him. Cat didn't say anything at first. She wasn't sure she could even come up with a word or phrase to describe what they had just experienced. It had left her unable to even think for a moment or two.

Then, she closed her eyes and kissed his neck. They both were damp from their exertion and, in that moment, it all felt right. The two of them, waking up to mind-altering sex, and now, in the quiet time together. Perfect.

"Well, good morning to you, Drew."

There was silence, then he started to chuckle. "Good morning."

They lay like that for a few minutes before he said, "I guess we need to get ready for work."

"Yeah," she said with a sigh. For the first time in a long time, she just wanted to lounge in bed. She lifted herself off the bed and smiled at him.

"Anytime you want to wake me up like that, you are definitely welcomed to."

"Promise?"

"Uh, yeah. I mean, I might be dead by the end of it, but at least I'll have died a decent death."

He shook his head, and tugged her down for a kiss. It was long and wet, and unbelievably sweet. When she pulled back, she felt the sting of tears in her eyes. She tried to blink them away, to make sure he didn't see them; but, as usual, he was too fast for her.

"Don't."

"Don't want to be with you in the morning?" she asked trying to joke, but this morning, he wasn't in that kind of mood apparently.

"I'm talking about the tears. You don't ever have to pretend with me, Cat. I think you're the most amazing woman."

"Drew."

"What? I know you better than you think I do."

That was what she was worried about.

"And there is one thing you are not and that is weak."

"How do you know that is what I was thinking?"

"I just do. You are strong and brilliant, and don't let anyone ever tell you any different."

It was probably the sweetest thing that anyone had ever told her. The damned burning was back, and when she blinked, a tear escaped. He leaned up and licked it from her cheek.

"You know, you can be fragile with me, right?"

"I'm not fragile."

"Oh, Cat, you are one of the most fragile people I know. It is something that makes you amazing. People don't see it, but I do. All that strength on the outside, but I know, inside, you hurt just like the rest of us. It doesn't make you weak. It makes you fucking strong. As soon as you can accept that, you'll understand how I see you."

"I don't think I ever will understand that."

"I know," he said. "I love you, Cat."

"No."

He chuckled. "Yes, I do. I mean, I've had a crush on you for years, but I never thought it through. I think the time apart taught me something about myself, about you. We needed it, we needed to make sure that we could stand on our own. But now, I'm ready to stand *with* you. I want to be by your side, I want to protect you from all evil, and I am always going to stand behind you to back you up. You can count on me."

"Drew," she said as her vision wavered.

"I didn't mean to make you cry. I just wanted you to know how I felt about you. About us."

"I'm not sure what to say."

He shrugged. "You don't have to say anything at all. Just accept that I love you, and one day, we'll figure out how to go from here."

"I…"

"You do not have to tell me anything at all. I wasn't looking for an answering declaration, and I didn't want to make you think that I expect anything in return. I just needed you to know."

She opened her mouth, but he put his fingers on her lips. "Don't answer. Don't worry. When you're ready, we'll talk it through."

She sighed. "Okay. How did you get so smart?"

"My mom says it's because of her. Dad agrees when she's in earshot. How about we take a quick shower and get ready to go in?"

"Sounds like a plan," she said.

He leaned up and kissed her again. Then, he rolled off the bed, picked her up and walked around the bed to the bathroom.

"No fooling around, either. We're already running late."

"Of course not," he said, but she heard the laughter in his voice, and she knew he was lying.

But for once, she wasn't going to worry about schedules, or what was expected of her. She was going to take a shower with a man who loved her and she was going to enjoy it.

Drew wasn't even feeling guilty for making them a little late for work. It was worth it to see Cat so happy. It wasn't until that moment in bed when he saw her fight the tears that he knew what to say to her. She needed to know exactly how much she meant to him. Now that she did, he felt even more powerful. The connection that had seemed so tenuous just a few days ago, now felt solid. He hoped she remembered what he had told her. If not, he would simply remind her.

"You know, if you keep things like that up, I might just lose my job. And you could lose yours," Cat said, as he held the door open for her.

He couldn't fight the smile that curved his lips and, why should he? He'd had the most amazing night, followed by a mind-blowing morning. That alone was enough to make him smile. But the fact he could do it all over again, that was what had him grinning. She had put her hair up in a sassy ponytail and was wearing the same basic uniform as always. Cargo pants, TFH shirt, and boots.

"Are you listening to me?"

He nodded his head. "Yeah, but you might want to keep your voice down."

"Why?"

"I thought you wanted to keep this only between us?"

She frowned at him as she pushed open the door to the conference room. She stepped inside and then turned to face him. "Like that matters. They all know anyway."

He glanced over her head and saw that everyone was either seated or standing around the conference table. Well, everyone but Charity, who was habitually late.

"Something's up," he murmured.

Cat turned around, then started in the direction of the crowd. "What's up?"

Del stood in front of the table blocking their view. His expression varied between anger and worry. That was enough to have Drew freaking out a little. Del rarely showed his emotions. "We had a delivery this morning. Early. Adam got here before six, and it was waiting for him."

Cat placed a hand on each of her hips and looked up at their boss. "What is it? A body part?"

A feeling of dread started to fill him. There had been one thing that had been delivered to each of the murder victims; and if he was right, Cat was going to have a fit.

"No. Seems Drew has picked up an admirer," Del said. He stepped aside and, there on the table, was a glass vase filled with red roses.

"It's addressed to you," Adam said.

Drew nodded and walked closer.

"Don't touch it," Charity yelled out as she came

running across the conference room floor toward the crowd. She had her lab coat on and was putting on a pair of blue latex gloves.

"I wasn't going to." He saw his name on the outside of the card. He looked up at Adam. "The name of the person who sent it?"

"No, and from what we can tell, there is no sign of where it came from either."

"I have the security recording, if you want to pull it up," Charity said.

Drew nodded and hit the buttons. They all watched as a person walked down the street, then turned up the pathway that lead to TFH headquarters. Whoever it was wore a hoodie, jeans, and sneakers. Because the person had pulled the hood up over her head, there was no telling who it was. Hell, there was no telling if it was a woman. It could have been a small guy. One who was smart enough to hide their face from the camera.

Charity took hold of the card, opening it and reading it. She turned the card over.

*You are mine. Now and forever.*

# CHAPTER NINETEEN

Drew tried to find comfort from being in Charity's lab. It had always been a place to come for comradery and laughter. It was also a place to come for support.

"So, you want to tell me why you and Cat came in to work together?" Charity asked, as she punched the buttons and started running the fingerprint she'd found. He knew that was the main reason she had invited him down to her lab to help.

"No. Not really."

They stared at each for a very long minute. Charity had always claimed to be able to crack any man and, for the most part, he believed her. There was one thing more important than that though. It was the promise he'd made to Cat. She didn't want the whole office to know about them just yet, and he wouldn't be the one who blurted it out.

Finally, she let out a "Dammit. Why don't you just tell me what's going on?"

He smiled.

"Oh, I'm going to make you pay for this. Even though TJ said I needed to leave you alone."

"Smart man, TJ."

"Oh, you all stick together. And that sucks."

It was always best to distract Charity. If she started to rant about something, there was a good chance she would never shut up about it. The one thing that could pull her focus away was work.

"That's a good print you have there."

She glanced at the screen. "Almost a full fingerprint, so they weren't *that* smart."

"And since none of the previous ones were recovered, maybe she thought it would end up in the trash. Maybe she just didn't worry about it."

"You think it is this woman you had the date with?"

He shrugged. "Not sure. She didn't seem that scary when we had the date. Although, she did make a joke about being a serial killer."

"She did?"

"Yeah, it was in reference to her parents, how they acted like moving to Oahu was horrible."

"Huh. That's interesting."

"Yeah. I remember it because it seemed so natural to throw out there. Truthfully, she could have just been joking. I guess we need to find out before my date tonight."

"How does Cat feel about you dating this woman?"

"What do you mean? She told me to make another date. I was just following orders. Plus, it isn't a real date. This is a work date."

She rolled her eyes. "You're being mean."

"You have to be sneakier than that to get me to screw up."

She shook her head. "I guess I'll let it go...for now. Although, that sentence pretty much proves my hypothesis."

He decided to ignore that comment. "All you have is the fingerprint?"

"Yes, and if the fingerprints aren't in the system, we can't find anything, but there is always a chance."

As soon as she said that, her computer pinged. The

woman was kind of eerie with her timing.

"We have a match," she said, and he hurried over with her to look. When they saw the name, they both stood there for a moment taking it all in.

"Holy moly," she muttered.

"You said a mouthful."

"I want him off the case," Cat said.

She was in Del's office, alone with him. After the meeting, Del had said they needed to talk. Adam had left to track down the information to see if Lana Cho was somehow connected to the flower delivery. Everyone else had scattered.

They had been going round and round for fifteen minutes. She had tried to come up with all kinds of reasons for Drew not to go on the date that night. She knew it was unprofessional, but she really didn't care. She didn't want Drew anywhere near this.

Del studied her as she paced back and forth. He had said very little, just countering her arguments with sound answers. It was annoying.

"There's no reason for that."

He said it calmly, as if he had just told her about the weather. It was frustrating.

She stopped and looked out over the deserted conference room. She couldn't seem to draw her gaze away from where the flowers had been sitting on the conference table. Charity had taken them downstairs for analyzing, and to determine if there were any fingerprints on the vase or card. Rage and fear tangled together in her gut. She should have never allowed him to be involved with the case. This was all her fault. Drew wasn't built for this. He was a geek, a man who shouldn't be out in the field.

"No reason? He could get killed."

"No, there is no reason to pull him. You're letting your emotions take over. I need to you to stay focused."

His voice was a bit sterner than usual, and she knew she had disappointed her boss. She didn't care, Drew was too important to her. She couldn't risk losing him just now after she had gotten him back.

She turned to face him. "I *am* focused."

After a long study, he shook his head. "No, you aren't. I know exactly what you're feeling."

"I don't think you do."

"Don't you remember when Emma wanted to go taunt a sadistic serial killer? Yeah, I see that you do. I understand what you are thinking, but the truth is, you don't have to worry. We can keep him safe, and besides, maybe Charity will find something."

"I don't like it."

"Of course, you don't. You're in love with him."

Even just hearing the words sent anxiety racing through her. "I do not."

Del chuckled. "Face it, Kalakau. You're hooked. You wouldn't have done anything so inappropriate as have a relationship with a fellow employee otherwise."

"There are no rules against it."

"No, but during an investigation like this, you know it's a little sketchy."

She opened her mouth to argue, but he held up his hand.

"I don't want to have an argument about this. Like I said, I don't have much room to talk. But I need you to understand what's at stake here. He has a serial killer who has killed at least four other people zeroed in on him. Taking him off the case isn't going to make her change her mind. You just leave him exposed."

Just hearing her thoughts expressed out loud left her feeling a little queasy. She knew it was true, but she desperately wanted him away from the danger. He had already been shot once. She couldn't handle him being hurt a second time.

Before she could answer the boss, Del's phone rang. He picked it up.

"Yeah." He listened for a while. "Are you sure?"

There was a lot of loud talking on the other end of the line, and even as stressed as she was, Cat couldn't help but smile. Charity didn't like when you questioned her results.

"Fine. Yeah. Cat's here. I'll tell her." He hung up. "You have a suspect to pull in."

"Who?"

"Lana Cho."

MELISSA SCHROEDER

# CHAPTER TWENTY

Drew stood outside of the interview room, staring through the one-sided mirror. Lana looked much like she had the night they went out together. Neat, kind of cute. She was dressed in scrubs, since they had pulled her out of work for the interview. He just couldn't see her as a killer. At the moment, her eyes kept moving around the room, as if looking, hoping for some kind of intervention. Maybe she was wondering if it was all a bad dream.

He couldn't blame her. He had watched Cat interrogate her for thirty minutes before Lana had asked for her attorney. Now the young woman sat there with an expression of loathing on her face. He didn't know if it was because she got caught, or if she was innocent. Even knowing that looks could be deceiving, he just couldn't picture her strangling a man to death.

"Hey," Marcus called out as he walked down the hall. "You have a visitor in the waiting area."

"A visitor?"

"Yeah, I think Elle said it was your mom. She's talking to her right now, but I know the woman wanted to talk with you."

Great. This was all he needed today. There was a good chance his mother was there only to try and gather up gossip.

"Okay. Nothing's going on here anyway."

"Still hasn't cracked?" Marcus asked as he stood beside Drew and took in the scene.

Drew shook his head. "Asked for her lawyer, so Cat is just doing a stare down with her."

"Cho doesn't look all that much like a serial killer."

"What do you mean? Because she's a woman?"

"No. Believe me, I understand women can be lethal, so it isn't that. It is her demeanor. All the ones I've seen after their arrest are usually cold, and act as if they are annoyed. The other kind are the true crazies who are ranting and raving about everything. They want to profess their manifesto or whatever."

"Yeah, that is what has gotten me confused. She seems more frightened than anything else. Which might just be an act. If she is a true sociopath, there is a chance she's playing another part."

"True," Marcus said nodding. "This could be awhile."

"Yeah, I'll go talk to my mom. Otherwise, she might corner someone else."

As he turned to leave, Marcus asked, "So, no helping me with the pool we have going about you and Cat?"

"No help," he said with a chuckle.

He walked down the hall thinking about what Marcus had said. From the beginning, he had doubts about Lana. She seemed to be exactly what she presented to the world. Hard working and sweet. But then, some of the most vicious serial killers were considered nice and quiet. That is, until something set the killer off. An explosion of violence would follow. This crime fit that type. Months went by without any murders, then one would pop up. Lana could be one of those types.

He found his mother sitting with Elle in the waiting area.

"Mom, what are you doing here? Is there anything wrong?"

"No," she said, shaking her head. "Just wanted to stop by and see you. And see Elle, of course."

His mother was approaching sixty, but didn't look a day over forty. She had recently cut her hair shorter, and she was sporting a Hawaiian Warriors T-shirt today. His mother was an avid supporter of the women's volleyball team at the university.

She stood so he could give her a kiss on the cheek. Then, as usual, she rubbed away the lipstick mark.

"I'm headed back down," Elle said. "I really enjoyed talking to you. You should stop by more often."

"I should, but someone doesn't like when I do that," his mother said, gesturing her head in his direction. "Just remember what I said."

"I will, Mrs. Franklin."

Once they were alone, he smiled at his mother. "What did you tell her?"

"She's going to have a boy. Easy to see with the way she is carrying. I hope you aren't too busy."

"No, I was just watching Cat interrogate a suspect."

"Oh, is this the woman who has been murdering her dates?"

"How did you hear about that?"

"It's all over the news. And, I might have talked to Mrs. Kalakau about it."

Damn. Cat wasn't going to be happy about that.

"That's why you stopped by?"

"What?" she asked, widening her eyes and trying to look innocent. He wasn't fooled. "I just came by to see you. It's been so long."

"I was at your house on Sunday." He shook his head. "Admit it. You came here to ask about me and Cat."

"I...okay, yes. She came in and said she saw you two at Cat's house early in the morning."

"Yeah."

"Do you want to tell me anything?"

"No."

"Andrew Franklin."

He couldn't help but smile. "Mom, listen, I know you want to meddle, but this isn't the time. We are about to wrap up this case. I'll talk to you this weekend about Cat and me, but right now, it isn't a good idea. It is kind of crazy today around here."

She studied him for a long minute. He wondered now what she and Mrs. Kalakau had talked about. Both of them were domineering in their own ways. Together, they could screw up the entire thing.

"Okay. But know that I want a full accounting. Can you tell me about this case?"

"A little bit. I went undercover."

She frowned. "I don't like that."

He shook his head. "I only pretended to date women. Well, *a* woman, there was only the one."

"You dated a woman under false pretenses? I raised you better than that."

"It was for a case."

"Still."

"She's a serial killer, mom. Or, she could be. They are figuring that out right now."

"And this service you used?"

"Premiere Connections."

Then his phone went off. As if on cue, it was Premiere Connections.

"Let me get this." He clicked his phone on. "Hello?"

"Mr. Franklin, this is Alice, you remember, the owner of PC."

He frowned at the familiarity. "Yes, of course."

"I was wondering if you could come by. We've had a problem with your account."

"My account?"

"Yes, we've had a hiccup, and I need to get all your paperwork redone. I don't want to suspend your service, but we will have to if I can't get this cleared up."

It seemed like an odd request, but the case still wasn't

closed. He needed to continue to play the part. "Let me check with my boss, but I should be able to swing by there."

"Thank you so much. I look forward to seeing you," she said, her voice softening over the words. Very odd.

When he hung up, he looked at his mother, who was studying him.

"The case."

"What about it?" she asked.

"The woman who runs the dating service called and said I needed to fill out more paperwork."

"Are you going to go?"

"Don't really have to."

"Why not?" she persisted. "The case is almost over, so there is no reason to pretend."

Del walked by and noticed he was talking to his mother. His boss opened the door and stuck his head in. "Howzit, Mrs. Franklin?"

"Come in, Captain Delano," she said, acting as if she owned the place and Del was a visitor. His mother had autocratic leanings that would make Mussolini blush.

"How are you doing today?" Del asked.

"Fine. That is until my son decided to ignore my request."

Del looked at him, then back at his mother. "He did something bad?"

"He made dates for this investigation."

"One date," Drew said, but his mother ignored him.

"And now he is going to ignore a call from the owner to come and work on some paperwork.

Again, Del looked at him. "She called you?"

"Yeah, said there was a glitch in the system, and I needed to redo some paperwork."

Del sighed. "I hate to say it, but you need to go then, even though it looks like the woman in interrogation is going to plea out."

"Yeah?"

Del nodded. "I'm hoping it is that easy. But, just in case, we need to keep up the ruse."

His mother smiled. "See. I told you."

He gave Del a nasty look, because Drew could tell from the smile Del was sporting, he knew exactly what he was doing.

"Well, I better go," his mother announced. "I've got some shopping to do also. Sunday dinner, yes?"

"Yes."

He watched as she walked out and then looked at Del. "That was crappy, boss."

"Aw, just go do it, because you can't lie for shit, Franklin," Del said as he started to head back into his office.

Drew walked back to interrogation where he found Cat standing outside the room.

"Hey," he said.

"I think we have her," Cat said.

"I heard her lawyer is talking plea bargain."

She nodded. "Yeah, so I think this one is tied up, thanks to you."

He smiled, then it faded. "I have to go by PC."

She glanced at him. "Why?"

"The owner called and said I needed to fix some paperwork. Del thinks I should keep up the ruse until we get everything settled here. I would have blown it off, but my mom told on me to Del."

"When did you talk to your mom?"

"Just now. Seems your mother stopped by the restaurant and said something to Mom about me being at your house."

"Huh."

"Yeah. I sidestepped that, but I got a Sunday invite, and it was clear she wanted you there as well. Anyway, Del gave me permission to go to PC, so I might as well do it now."

"You know, you could just wait. Or at least take

204

someone with you."

"Really? Because I am pretty sure that my mother already has reminders set to tell her to text me about it."

She chuckled. "You're a sweet man."

He grabbed her T-shirt and pulled her forward. "Yeah? Not sure I like that description."

"Well, you should," she said, rising to her tiptoes and brushing her mouth over his.

"I guess I will take it as a compliment," he said as she backed away. "I'm going over there now, then I'll text and see what's up with Lana."

"Cool. Be careful."

"Always," he said, then he leaned back in for a long kiss. "You be careful too."

He turned and walked away, wanting nothing more than to get this damned thing over with as soon as possible.

"I think it's odd that her lawyer wants to plea her out so fast," Cat said as she chewed on her thumbnail.

She hated the habit because it always made her think of her mother, who berated her for it. And, well, it was kind of disgusting in a way. But the truth was, she couldn't stop right now. Her nerves were wired tight, and she didn't know why. She would normally say it was the case, but there was something else bothering her. It was as if she forgot one bit of important information. It felt like an itch beneath her skin she couldn't seem to scratch.

"Yeah, it is weird," Adam agreed. "But maybe she wanted to have it over and done with."

She shrugged. She had been surprised about how fast the lawyer had said he wanted to make a deal. Most people would at least try to play hardball, but this guy did not. He just rolled over right away. Maybe he had something else to play with. There was always a chance there were other victims they did not know about. These people always looked for an angle to avoid the death penalty. That didn't matter in Hawaii though, because they didn't have the death penalty.

"I hear Drew went to PC?"

She nodded. "That Collins woman called and said he needed to get something fixed on his application."

Before he could respond, the lawyer tapped on the glass.

"I guess that's my cue."

"Need any help?" Adam asked.

She shook her head as she opened the door and went inside. Lana looked calmer, ready to take some more questioning.

"So, Ms. Cho, you want to tell me what you would like me to know? What is this plea that you two are interested in?"

"She will plead guilty to solicitation with immunity on the other thing."

Cat blinked. "What?"

"She wants immunity on leaving the flowers."

Cat looked at the woman, then at the lawyer. "What the hell are you talking about? She's being charged with murder."

"Because of the fingerprint on the card and envelope?"

She nodded. "Her car was seen in the area."

"Exactly. She was delivering the flowers."

"And this solicitation?"

"Through Premiere Connections. Ms. Cho is willing to help you your investigation with that."

Just as she opened her mouth, someone tapped on the window, hard. She tried to ignore it, but the tapping turned into banging.

"Excuse me for a second."

She rose from the chair and stepped out into the hallway. Charity was standing there with Adam. After she shut the door, Cat settled her hands on her hips and stared at the forensics tech.

"What the hell, Charity?"

"You need to read this," she said, waving the papers around. "I tried to call, but you know this is a dead zone."

She grabbed the papers. "What is this?"

"That is another name for Alice Collins. She was known in California as Alison Marks, in Arizona as Monica Sellers, and in Texas as Alicia Walters."

"Which one is her real name?"

"I haven't found that, but one thing I know is that there are murders in all those locations. Always wealthy men who used a dating service."

Her blood iced over as she started reading through the report. Without a word, she opened the door to the investigation room. "Ms. Cho, was it Alice Collins who sent you to place the flowers?"

Before her lawyer could stop her, she nodded.

The ramifications of that one little nod sent fear lancing through Cat. She left the room, slamming the door behind her. She started for the conference room, because she had to get to Drew.

"Call him," Adam said

She pulled out her phone and hit his number, straight to voicemail "Dammit, what a day to forget to charge."

"What?"" Charity said as she hurried behind them.

"Drew just left for PC and doesn't know he's meeting with the killer."

Drew walked down the sidewalk to PC and wondered why he was even bothering with this. Well, other than the boss told him to. He had a feeling that Lana Cho would plead out and all of this would be finished. He opened the door to Premiere Connections, and found it empty. There were no clients or employees, and the place was dark. There was a light on near the desk, but other than that, no sign of life. He fought against the icy finger that slid down his spine.

"Alice," he called out.

No answer. The entire office was devoid of sound. Even the PCs were silent.

"It's Drew Franklin. You called?"

Silence filled the air around him. There was a different atmosphere today. He had expected the place to be filled with other people. That had to be it.

"Ms. Collins?" he said, checking one more time.

He was about to turn to leave when he heard her speak.

"Yes," she said from the back area. "Do you mind coming back here?"

"Sure," he said, even though he was feeling a little creeped out. He didn't want her to know that, so he needed to fake it. Besides, it was probably because of the office being empty. He always found offices kind of weird at night.

He walked through the doorway to another darkened room. Creepier and creepier.

"Alice?"

Nothing. He stepped in further, then he heard a noise behind him. He turned, but not quick enough. Alice hit him over the head with something hard in her hand. He fell back, stumbling into a desk and then a chair. He hit his head on the table as he descended. The floor came rushing at him as everything around him faded to black.

# TANGLED PASSIONS

# CHAPTER TWENTY-ONE

Cat rode in the passenger seat, still trying to reach Drew, as Adam drove. The sirens were blaring and her nerves were strung tight.

Voicemail.

She hung up and tried to call again.

"Still nothing?" Adam asked.

"Of course, there's nothing. Would I be redialing again if he picked up?"

Then she realized how screechy she'd just sounded.

"I'm sorry."

Adam shook his head. "Don't worry. I completely understand."

Again, it went straight to voicemail. "Jesus, this is horrible."

Her fingers shook as she hit the redial again. And it was all her fault. She had been against this from the beginning, but she should have been more forceful. She should have insisted on someone else. Drew wasn't ready for this kind of work. He could already be hurt, or dying. She couldn't think of anything other than getting there and saving him. Every damn thing, her fault.

"Don't," Adam ordered.

"What?"

"Don't blame yourself."

She didn't say anything to that, but she got a text. Graeme, Del, and Marcus were on their way. They would, at least, have backup after they arrived.

"The rest of the team is right behind us."

Adam nodded as he swerved around a sedan and then turned down the street that lead to PC. He had barely parked the vehicle when Cat jumped out of it and onto the street. Before she could take off, Adam grabbed her and pulled her back.

"Stop," he ordered.

She tried to struggle free, but he gave her a gentle shove and stepped in front of her.

"We have no idea what's happening in there. She could be hurting him right now," she said.

She shouldn't be freaking out, but there was no way she could stop herself. Not right now, not when she could lose Drew.

"Even more reason to get our heads together and make sure we don't go charging in there." He leaned down into her face. "You will get control or I will take over the operation, do you understand me?"

She closed her eyes and called on every bit of control she could find within her. Cat knew she needed to keep it cool. Drew's life depended on it. Adam was right. If she went in there with guns blazing and looking for blood, she could end up getting Drew killed.

She sucked in a deep breath then released it slowly. When she opened her eyes, she was centered and ready to go in.

Adam nodded. "Good. Let's get going. I'll follow your lead."

With a renewed sense of purpose, she started on her way. It was time to go save her man.

A slap to the face woke Drew up. He blinked, trying to focus on his surroundings. He moved his head and instantly regretted it. An explosion of pain rattled his brain.

"You shouldn't move," a soft voice said.

"Alice?"

She stepped into the light. She looked much the same at first, but when his eyes finally focused on her, he realized she didn't look quite like when he'd first met her. Her clothes were wrinkled and stained. Saying that her hair looked unkempt would be an understatement. It looked as if she had been rolling around in an alley.

This woman was not well. The best way to bide his time, so he could come up with a way to escape, was to act like he was concerned. Which he was, because she looked like she had gone completely over the edge.

"Alice. Are you okay? What happened to you?"

She snorted. "Like you don't know."

She stepped closer, and he could finally see her eyes. Good lord. There was no sanity left.

"I really don't," he said and tried to lift his arms. That's when he realized that she'd tied them to the chair with rope.

"It took a lot of work to get you in that position. I would hate to have to hit you again, so stop doing that."

He stopped struggling and started thinking of another tactic. One that would at least stretch out time or get her distracted. It would be hours before Cat would notice he was missing or start to worry. No one at work expected to see him. This was a worse case kind of scenario. Distraction would work best, in his opinion. Playing to her vanity might work best.

"So, you're the one who sent the flowers?"

She smiled. "Yes. Did you like them?"

Lord, she was definitely pupule. "Yes. They were

amazing."

She clapped her hands. "I'm so glad you liked them. I had Lana drop them off."

"You know Lana?"

"Yes. She's a customer." She leaned closer and it was evident Alice hadn't bathed or brushed her teeth in a long time. "Well, she also works for me."

He blinked, trying to make sense of the conversation. "Works?"

"Yes, for the service."

Service? What the hell was she talking about? Then, the memory of the initial rundown of the investigation hit him.

"Premiere Collections is an escort service?"

"Yes. Well, sort of. Some of the dates are just that, but a lot are like yours. It gives that sense of a real business, and it takes the authorities forever to figure it out."

"You've done this before?"

She nodded as she walked over to the desk and poured a drink. The liquid was brown, and he was assuming it was probably whiskey or bourbon. That could go either way. It could make her sloppy, or mean. When she slammed the glass down, he saw the gun next to it on the desk. That must have been what she hit him with. That didn't bother him as much as the red scarf did.

"Yes, I have done it before, but this place…it was easier. I thought I would be here just a few months, but I realized after I got here, that it was a goldmine. It's amazing that so many people on such a small island can keep so many secrets."

"And so you set up the business, and then you were going to go to…"

"Japan. They don't even mind there. Or maybe Australia where it's legal in some places to run an escort service. Doesn't matter. I stayed here."

"Why?"

"I told you," she said, her voice rising. "With the tourists in and out of here, it made it easy…so easy."

"And, being smart, you stayed."

For a moment, she stood still. Then she approached him. The smile transformed into an insane grin.

"I knew you would understand."

Cat had her gun out as she approached the door cautiously. Adam followed her lead.

"Is there a back way out of there?" Adam asked over the communications device.

"I'm not sure. I'm assuming there is because it's a shopping center. Why don't you try to check it out?"

"Copy that," he said. "Remember, keep your cool, Kalakau."

"I've got nerves of steel," she said.

It irritated her that people kept telling her to remain calm. She was sure that the boss got the same warnings about Emma, but she was damned sure it didn't sound like an order. She knew they meant well, but it was screwing with her concentration.

"When it's someone you care about, it fucks up your focus. Just remember, the important thing is to keep your head screwed on straight so we all make it out alive."

"We have no idea if she's armed or if she even knows what's going on."

She sensed his nod before he left to look for a back entrance.

Although, looking at the situation now, it was odd. The lights on the front of the store were out. Even at night, they should be on. As she made her way to the door, her pulse ratcheted up another notch. Sweat rolled down her back.

She made it to the door and was surprised to find it unlocked. With a slow and easy movement, she opened it and waited. No sounds came from inside, and no chime sounded, so she was safe, for now. Maybe they were overreacting, maybe Collins hadn't figured out they were onto her. She slipped through the opening, careful to cover all the corners.

"I thought I would never get caught here. And I thought you were truthful."

"Truthful?" Drew asked.

Relief filtered through her and for once quick moment, she sent up a prayer. He was safe. For now.

"You said you found out about me because of the investigation, but you were part of it. Then you had to take up with that whore."

"I think you need to watch your language."

Dammit, of course, Drew would get pissy about that. She heard the smack and knew Alice had hit him. Her finger itched to use the trigger, but she held back. The need to rush in there and save him grew with each step she took. But she knew she needed to wait, to assess the situation. Still, it irritated the living crap out of her.

She thanked the good Lord for the carpet on the floor, which kept her footsteps quiet. She kept her back to the wall as she followed the light from around the corner. The sound of voices seemed to be coming from the same direction, so it was a safe bet that they were together.

"I told you before not to contradict me. Men are always doing that."

"And that's why you make them pay?"

"That and because they are the lesser beast. You know, I thought maybe you were different. You were nerdy and sweet and cute. And I thought you would be…I don't know, faithful."

"I *am* faithful."

Cat peeked around the corner and found them. Collins had him tied to a chair, and she was standing in front of him. There was a light on the table beside Collins. Cat saw the liquor, the gun, and the red scarf.

"Really? Because you were dating Lana and fucking that bitch detective."

She ground her teeth together when Collins called her a bitch. It took all of her control not to rush in there and beat the shit out of her. Then, there was a loud bang at the back of the store. Apparently, Adam had found the back door. He banged on it a couple of times.

"What is that?"

"I don't know," Drew said quietly. "It's not my store."

Collins muttered something and walked toward the rear of the store. Cat knew that this was the perfect time to get Drew out of there. As quietly as she could, she hurried to him. When she finally saw his face, she growled. He had been hit at least once with something heavy. Blood dripped down his face, and he had a split lip.

"Took you long enough, Kalakau," he whispered.

"Stuff it, Franklin, or I'll leave you with that crazy bitch," she said as she set her gun down beside him and started to work on his restraints.

"God, I love you."

"Yeah, yeah, I love you too. Now shut up or she'll come back and catch us."

"Oh, I think it's too late," Collins said from behind her.

Cat turned, ready to strike and found Collins with a gun.

"Oh, there you are. Well, seeing how I'm the bitch you were talking about earlier, I thought maybe I had a right to him."

"No. He's mine. The only sad thing I didn't get to do was sleep with him. I have an idea that he is quite the stallion."

"So, this isn't the same as the others?"

She shook her head. "For so long, no one noticed here. Of course, I had to be a bit more selective. I had to watch them longer, make sure they had no friends nearby, no one who would see me come and go. Took forever for Branson's kids to leave the island, and he was easy. Really easy. But then, along came Drew. He made me believe, you know. He was so sweet…so real."

"He still is," she said inching her way over to fully shield him from Collins.

"No. He went out on a date with Lana and just gave her a kiss goodnight. And I thought that proved it. But no, it was because of you. But then, all men cheat."

"They don't. Drew doesn't."

Collins snorted and the barrel of the gun wavered. She was so ready to crack, she was shaking. Cat didn't know if it were anger or fear. Then, before she knew what was happening, Drew came up out of the chair. Collins freaked and shot the gun, but the bullet went over their heads. Cat knew that she had to get to the other woman before she had a chance to fire again. Rushing forward, she tackled her. The gun went off again right before they both hit the floor. They rolled over the floor, and Cat hit her head on the desk before she gained control. Stars appeared before her eyes, and she blinked them away the best she could.

She wrapped her hand around Collins' wrist, and beat her hand against the floor until she dropped the gun. Then Cat straddled the other woman. Collins reached up and tried to scratch Cat's face, but she easily batted her hands away. When she tried to hit Cat, it was the last straw. She punched Collins with a good right hook, completely knocking her out.

Cat stood up just as TFH and HPD came pouring into the room. As she turned around, the room began to spin a little, but she ignored it. She saw Drew then, who still had one hand tied to the chair. He was furiously trying to undo the restraint so she hurried forward to help

"Here," she said, as she slipped her fingers beneath the rope and undid the knot. When he was free, he grabbed her and pulled her against him.

"Damn, I thought we were both goners," he said.

She should've said something, but she was trying to keep from throwing up on him.

"Cat?" he asked as he pulled her back. "Damn, you look pale."

"I'm fine. Don't worry. You're the one bleeding."

Adam came up behind her, and she heard Del barking orders.

"How are you doing?" Adam asked.

"Fine, just a little woozy from the hit on the head," she said. She would not faint. She had never fainted before, and she most definitely wasn't going to start now. "We need to get Drew to the hospital to be checked out."

"I'm fine."

"You're freaking bleeding," she said, then had to press her lips together.

"And so are you," Adam pointed out.

"What?"

She raised her hand to the back of her head and found blood. "Well, shit."

"Not just there," Adam said. Looks like she nicked you with a bullet."

"Positively going to the hospital," Drew said.

She glared at him. "Right back at ya."

"It's a date," he said with a smile, then it faded. "Cat, are you okay?"

"Yes," she said as the room started to spin. "I just need to sit down."

She moved toward the chair Drew had been sitting in, but she never reached it. She felt herself pitching forward, and she heard Drew call her name.

Then she heard nothing at all.

# TANGLED PASSIONS

# CHAPTER TWENTY-TWO

It took hours to get through all the mess at the hospital. Drew was examined and questioned. They determined right away that he didn't have a concussion. All the while, he couldn't get an answer about Cat's condition. They said he would only be told after he had been examined.

The nurse came in just moments later.

"Mr. Franklin, I hear you want to know about Officer Kalakau."

"Agent."

"Okay, agent. She's fine. They cleaned her wound. Just a flesh wound. No stitches. She's getting an MRI right now, then we can update you again."

"Thank you. I don't have to stay in here, do I?"

"No. Here are your discharge papers. If you go out to the waiting room, we'll come and give you another update."

He thanked the nurse and made his way out to the waiting room. After he called his mother—because he knew that someone would have told her— he called Charity

"Hey, what are you doing calling here?" Charity said. "Shouldn't you be getting your brain checked?"

"They checked me out, and I'm fine. What's going on there?"

"Adam has been interrogating Collins. She's been

linked to at least three other murders. I'm sure there will be more. She keeps spouting off about the demon men who have ruined her life."

"Damn. Did you find anything else out about her?"

"Her real name is Francine Dumont. Comes from money, or did, until her father lost it. He was running some kind of Ponzi scheme when it all imploded about twenty years ago. Then, she disappeared off the map. She was sixteen at the time, but there is no record of her going to school or going to the university. They are still trying to piece it together, but apparently, Francine didn't handle going from Greenwich, Connecticut to Boston."

"I can imagine."

"Worse, her father didn't suffer the same fate as she and her mother. He ran off with funds he embezzled, with his mistress, to Moldova. So, I kind of understand her hatred of men."

"Damn."

"How's Cat?"

He sighed and rubbed his temple. He might not have a concussion, but he had one hell of a headache brewing. "I'm waiting for them to come get me. She just had a flesh wound, but they need to get it cleaned and check out her head."

"But she's okay?"

"Yes."

"Good, because I am getting damned sick of all of us going to the hospital. We need a break"

"I agree wholeheartedly."

"Oh, wait, here's Adam."

The phone jostled around as Charity handed it over to the second-in-command. "Drew, howzit?"

"Doing okay. I don't have a concussion, and I'm waiting to hear about Cat."

"The boss should be there soon. He wanted to make sure everything here was taken care of, and he had to call Mrs. Kalakau."

As if on cue, Cat's mother came bursting into the ER. "And...she's here. Let me let you go. I need to talk with her and make sure she knows what's going on."

"Gotcha."

After hanging up, he made a beeline for Cat's mother, who was hassling one of the clerks.

"Ms. Kalakau," he said, and she turned toward him. She had been loud and rude, but the moment he saw her face, he knew it was out of fear.

"Andrew." She rushed over to him. "Is Catherine safe?"

"Yes. They are just cleaning her wound and making sure she doesn't have a concussion."

She let out a sigh of relief, then she studied him. "You were hurt too?"

He nodded, as he guided her over to a seat. "Before Cat got there."

She sat down with a grunt. "This is the reason she should *not* do this work. She needs to be safe."

"I can't agree with that."

"You don't think she needs to be safe?"

"No, I can't agree that she shouldn't do this work. If it wasn't for her, I wouldn't be alive."

She studied him for a long moment. "That is one good thing. Still, she must quit. This isn't the profession for her."

"Mrs. Kalakau, I have to humbly disagree, and if you can't see this is what she was born to do, then you're not looking close enough."

When she said nothing, he continued.

"She's excellent at her job and, thanks to her, there's a serial killer behind bars. As I said, this is what she was born to do, and if you truly loved her, you would accept it. And you need to learn to accept her for who she is. She hates that you don't get along. She hasn't said anything to me, but I know it hurts her that you aren't close anymore."

Again, she quietly studied him, her face void of

expression. "You think you know her better than I do?"

"I know her, and I love her for who she is. I can't see her doing anything else and being happy. You need to accept that, or your relationship will never be right. She's an amazing agent, and you need to support her."

Before her mother could respond, a nurse approached them. "Mrs. Kalakau? You can see your daughter now."

He stood up to follow, but the nurse asked him, "Are you related?"

He shook his head.

"I can only let family back, but they will have her up in her room soon enough."

His heart almost stopped. They had told him it was nothing serious. "She's being admitted?"

"Just for observation as a precaution."

He nodded as he released a long breath. "Thanks."

Cat's mother looked at him one last time, then turned away to follow the nurse. He sat back down and tried to order himself not to worry. Being kept overnight wasn't necessarily a sign that something was wrong. And he would get to see her soon enough.

Five minutes later, Del and Emma arrived, and they made a beeline for him.

"Drew," Emma said as she reached down to hug him. "Are you okay?"

He was so astounded by the unusually friendly gesture from Emma, it took him a second to answer. She wasn't a woman who made big displays of emotion, especially in public.

"I'm fine."

She gave him another squeeze, then straightened.

"How is she?" Del asked.

"Looks like everything is fine, but they are keeping her overnight."

"Why aren't you back there?" Emma asked.

"I'm not family. They said she was going up to her room in a while."

Emma looked at Del.

"What?" he asked.

"Go fix it," she ordered, as she gestured to the on-duty nurse.

And he knew Del would do it. Even if Del didn't head up an elite law enforcement team, he could have gotten Drew back there. Del had the ultimate 'don't fuck with me' attitude, and it scared most people who didn't know him.

"No," Drew said. "Her mother is back there right now."

"Are you sure?" Emma asked. "I think you should be back there."

He smiled, even as his headache seemed to get worse with each minute he sat there.

"Yes. I think they have some things to discuss."

She sat down beside him and touched the bandage on his forehead. "I'm glad you're okay. This is getting really old."

Del smiled. "I agree with that."

"Me three," he said.

"Want some coffee or a drink?" Del asked.

Drew opened his mouth to say no, but Emma interrupted him.

"Some water. Get him some water," Emma said.

He frowned as he watched his boss weave through all the milling people in the ER waiting room.

"Why did you do that?"

She sighed. "He has to have something to do or he'll go crazy. Adam is already handling the interrogation. He also wants to hit something because this happened. It's the Alpha in him. He wants to punish someone for you and Cat being hurt. Giving him a chore distracts him."

He smiled. "You sure do know your husband."

"Damned right I do. Now, about this wager on you and Cat."

"No comment."

"You suck. But I still like you."

Cat was lying in bed, still in the ER, when her mother was shown in. Damn, she wasn't in the mood for this. Her head still throbbed since they wanted to keep her pain meds at a minimum until after they had the results of the MRI.

"Catherine," her mother said as she approached the bed.

She studied her mother. Cat had expected her to be angry, but instead, she saw tears in her mother's eyes.

"Mom." It was all she could say around the lump in her throat.

Her mother cleared her throat. "How are you feeling?"

"Like I hit my head and got shot."

Her mother laughed, but it ended with a sob. She wasn't sure just what to do. Her mother had never been one to cry, *ever*. Even when their father had died, her mother did not cry. At least not in front of her girls.

"Don't cry."

"I'm sorry," she said pulling a tissue out of her purse. "I didn't mean to cry. Not here."

"It's okay. I understand."

She wiped away the tears and blew her nose. "I thought my world had ended today when I got the call from Commander Delano."

Tears burned the backs of Cat's eyes, and she tried to blink them away, but it did no good. They spilled down her cheeks.

"You know how much I need you to be safe."

She nodded. "I know."

"No," her mother said as she stepped closer, then sat down on the bed. "You don't. You think it is because I expect so much out of you, but it's because if you're there, I know I can make it. You're tough, and you make me believe I can handle anything."

"Mom, you *can* handle anything. You raised four girls by yourself."

"Yes, but you know I couldn't have done it without you. My rock. Ever since you were little, you were always there to help, and now I see what it caused."

"What?"

Her mother sighed. "You need your own life. You need to be happy."

"I am happy. I love my work."

Her mother took another tissue from her purse and wiped Cat's tears. She hadn't done that since the day Cat's father had died.

"I didn't understand before," she said.

"Before today?"

Her mother shook her head. "Before your young man told me. He explained it all to me. He loves you very much."

Cat nodded. "Good, because I love him."

Her mother smiled, then took her hand. "I am not happy about this career of yours, and I will never understand it, but I will learn to accept it."

"Well, gee, that's a great gesture."

"Watch it," she said.

Cat chuckled. "Sure thing."

"He's a very special man, your Andrew."

She nodded. "Yeah. He's pretty damned special."

"So, tell me about this crazy woman who shot you."

She laughed and started to tell her mother what she knew about the case. And, for the first time in a long time, she could share laughter with her mother with none of the pain.

When she woke up the next morning, the only thing

Cat could think of was that she freaking hurt. Damn. And it had nothing to do with the gunshot wound, although that did sting. No, her head was pounding.

She blinked and tried to open her eyes. It took her a few tries, but her eyes finally focused. Carefully, she looked around the room and found Drew sitting beside her bed. She turned her head and white hot pain flashed through her brain, and then through her entire body.

"Fuck."

Her utterance jolted Drew awake. He blinked a few times, then focused on her.

"Hey, there," he said, getting up and walking to the bed. "Good to see you awake."

"Have you been here all night?"

He nodded. "Del sweet talked the nurses into letting me stay."

She licked her lips. They were dry and hurt like hell.

"Do you need some water?"

She nodded, then watched him as he poured some water into a cup with a straw. He walked over to her, sat on her bed, and helped her drink. The cool liquid slipped down her throat and gave her some relief. When she was finished, he set the cup on the bedside table.

"How are you feeling?"

"Like crap."

He chuckled.

"Well, I'm glad you have found amusement in my plight. What's going on with Collins?"

"Adam is working the issue. She's been tied to several other murders, and they are trying to track down all her aliases."

"How did I miss that?"

"How did we *all* miss that? Everyone had the same information."

"She was the one woman they each had in common. We didn't even pick up on that."

He nodded. "Looks like Lena is turning state's

evidence. Going to testify about the whole operation."

"I don't know how we missed that either. I didn't find anything big that would tell me she was hooking."

"She had student debt from college apparently. She'd paid it off and planned on working for just a few more months to save some money up."

"Well, damn. Again, another screw up."

He took hold of her hand and squeezed it. "We all did, but we knew it had to do with that dating service. Remember, HPD did a very involved investigation and couldn't find anything. Collins apparently has a world class mind when it comes to hiding money."

"I take it Alice Collins isn't her real name?"

He shook his head. "Nope. Francine Dumont. Came from a lot of money before he father lost it all. Charity is working on piecing her life together. She's been using aliases for probably close to twenty years."

"Good lord, no wonder none of us saw it. She must have been a teenager when she started."

"Sixteen from what Charity found. It all boiled down to a cheating father who abandoned them."

"Damn. Daddy issues."

He nodded and raised her hand to his mouth and kissed it. Then he closed his eyes and held their joined hands against his forehead. "Don't ever get shot again."

"It was just a flesh wound."

He opened his eyes. "Still, not again. I can't lose you."

She opened her mouth, but nothing came out. The emotion she heard in his voice shimmered through her as her vision wavered.

"Don't cry," he said, wiping her tears away.

"I don't want anything to happen to you, Drew. I'm trained for this, but you aren't. You're supposed to hang out with Elle and be safe. You've been injured twice on the job now."

"We are in complete agreement. We don't want anything to happen to each other." Then he kissed her hand again. "I love you."

She smiled through the tears. "I love you too."

He released a breath. "Oh, good, I thought you were going to tell me that one declaration you made didn't count."

She shook her head, then groaned. "Damn."

"They'll bring you some pain meds soon."

"Good." She sighed then looked at him. "I don't know when I realized it. Maybe it was today, or maybe it was last week. But somewhere along the way, you became part of me. Losing you would be too much. I..." she wiped fresh tears away. "I was scared for so long after you were shot. And that fear drove me away from you. I knew that if I stayed with you, I would be hurt."

"I wouldn't hurt you on purpose."

"No. Just the thought of losing you hurt, and when you were shot, well, I let my fears take over. If I stayed away, then I wouldn't get hurt. But I *was* hurting. Every damned day I saw you."

"Yeah, that was stupid."

"Drew."

"What? It *was* stupid. Think of all the fun we could have had over the last year."

She smiled. "Better late than never."

He leaned down and brushed his mouth over hers. "I guess proposing marriage right now would be tacky?"

She waited for the panic to set in, but instead, she felt a small jolt of joy. "Well, not right now. I think we need to get used to each other first. Just be us."

He smiled. "I like that idea. Just being us."

She raised her head slowly and kissed him. "Thank you, Drew."

"For what? You saved me."

"No. You saved me from myself. I love you."

He rolled his eyes. "Really, after you say that, I can't propose?"

She laughed. "No. But you can sit here and tell me you

love me, then tell me more about what's happened with the case overnight."

Drew smiled. "I do love you, Catherine Kalakau."

With the morning sun peeking through the blinds, he sat there, holding her hand, he told her what she wanted to know.

Thank you so much for reading Tangled Passions. I hope you enjoyed Drew and Cat's story. If you enjoyed the book, please think about leaving a review on your favorite online book retailer and tell your friends about the book.

Mel

# TANGLED PASSIONS

# ABOUT MELISSA SCHROEDER

From an early age, USA Today Bestselling author Melissa Schroeder loved to read. First, it was the books her mother read to her including her two favorites, *Winnie the Pooh* and the *Beatrix Potter* books. She cut her preteen teeth on *Trixie Belden* and read and reviewed *To Kill a Mockingbird* in middle school. It wasn't until she was in college that she tried to write her first stories, which were full of angst and pain, and really not that fun to read or write. After trying several different genres, she found romance in a Linda Howard book.

Since the publication of her first book in 2004, Melissa has had close to fifty romances published. She writes in genres from historical suspense to modern day erotic romance to futuristics and paranormals. Included in those releases is the bestselling Harmless series. In 2011, Melissa branched out into self-publishing with A Little Harmless Submission and the popular military spinoff, Infatuation: A Little Harmless Military Romance. Along the way she has garnered an epic nomination, a multitude of reviewer's recommended reads, over five Capa nods from TRS, three nominations for AAD Bookies and regularly tops the bestseller lists on *Amazon* and *Barnes & Noble*. She made the USA Today Bestseller list for the first time with her anthology The Santinis.

Since she was a military brat, she vowed never to marry military. Alas, fate always has her way with mortals. Her husband just retired from the AF after 20 years, and together they have their own military brats, two girls, and two adopted dog daughters, and is happy she picks where they live now.

Keep up with Mel online:
Facebook.com/melissashcroederfanpage
Twitter.com/melschroeder
Pinterest.com/melissaschro
Facebook.com/groups/harmlesslovers – Mel's private fan group!

# HARMLESS

A Little Harmless Sex
A Little Harmless Pleasure
A Little Harmless Obsession
A Little Harmless Lie
A Little Harmless Addiction
A Little Harmless Submission
A Little Harmless Fascination
A Little Harmless Fantasy
A Little Harmless Ride
A Little Harmless Secret
A Little Harmless Rumor

## THE HARMLESS PRELUDES

Prelude to a Fantasy
Prelude to a Secret
Prelude to a Rumor, Part One
Prelude to a Rumor, Part Two

## THE HARMLESS SHORTS

Max and Anna
Chris and Cynthia

## A LITTLE HARMLESS MILITARY ROMANCE

Infatuation

Possession
Surrender

## THE SANTINIS

Leonardo
Marco
Gianni
Vicente
A Santini Christmas
A Santini in Love
Falling for a Santini
One Night with a Santini
A Santini Takes the Fall
A Santini's Heart

## SEMPER FI MARINES

Tease Me
Tempt Me
Touch Me

## THE FITZPATRICKS
At Last

## TASK FORCE HAWAII

Seductive Reasoning
Hostile Desires
Constant Craving
Tangled Passions

## ONCE UPON AN ACCIDENT

An Accidental Countess
Lessons in Seduction
The Spy Who Loved Her


## THE CURSED CLAN

Callum
Angus
Logan


## BY BLOOD

Desire by Blood
Seduction by Blood

## BOUNTY HUNTER'S, INC

For Love or Honor
Sinner's Delight

## THE SWEET SHOPPE

Cowboy Up
Tempting Prudence

## LONESTAR WOLF PACK
The Alpha's Saving Grace

## CONNECTED BOOKS

The Hired Hand
Hands on Training

A Calculated Seduction
Going for Eight

## SINGLE TITLES

Grace Under Pressure
Telepathic Cravings
Her Mother's Killer
The Last Detail
Operation Love
Chasing Luck
The Seduction of Widow McEwan

## COMING SOON
The Boss (Entangled Publishing)
A Little Harmless Temptation
Fletcher
Wicked Temptations

CPSIA information can be obtained
at www.ICGtesting.com
Printed in the USA
LVOW07s2107010517
532858LV00003B/586/P